They hadn't been in love.

They'd been in lust, and she was all about lust in that moment. All about pleasure. For two weeks, he was here, the man who'd been the best sex of her life. She'd be a fool to run. She would enjoy him, and then she would say goodbye.

Starting with this kiss. The instant Jennifer's mouth touched Bobby's, he pulled her closer, taking her mouth, as if he feared she might change her mind. His mouth parted hers, intimately, full of demand. One of his hands tangled in her hair, the other slid up her back, pressing her close, molding her to all that delicious hard muscle. Her hands slid over his back as he pressed her against the car. Long, strong thighs entwined with hers.

Their kiss was...arousing. It made her thoughts spin and her heart race. Yet, still, he seemed unaffected, cool, confident, in control, with an edge that had always been Bobby and had only grown more frustratingly sexy with time and maturity.

"Peace offering," he said, obviously offering so much more....

Dear Reader,

Welcome to the Hotzone—The Texas Hotzone—where three ex-members of the Crazy Aces Special Forces team have opened a skydiving operation right outside of my hometown of Austin, Texas.

Jump Start is book one in the trilogy, and it is a story about finding what you've lost. And no, I'm not talking about your car keys, but rather the key to your heart. Which consequently, in *Jump Zone*, is going to require a whole lot of seduction by the hero, Bobby Evans, because this key is buried deep. Of course, he gets help in the form of a combination bachelor/bachelorette party and a game of truth-or-dare. Read onward to find out if his heroine, Jennifer Jones, chooses the truth or the dare, and just how hot things have to get to find that key.

I hope you enjoy *Jump Start*, and look for book two, *High Octane*, in March. Please visit me at www.lisareneejones.com.

Enjoy!

Lisa Renee Jones

Lisa Renee Jones

JUMP START

TORONTO • NEW YORK • LONDON
AMSTERDAM • PARIS • SYDNEY • HAMBURG
STOCKHOLM • ATHENS • TOKYO • MILAN • MADRID
PRAGUE • WARSAW • BUDAPEST • AUCKLAND

Recycling programs
for this product may
not exist in your area.

ISBN-13: 978-0-373-79594-9

JUMP START

Copyright © 2011 by Lisa Renee Jones

This edition published by arrangement with Harlequin Books S.A.

For questions and comments about the quality of this book please contact us at Customer_eCare@Harlequin.ca.

® and TM are trademarks of the publisher. Trademarks indicated with ® are registered in the United States Patent and Trademark Office, the Canadian Trade Marks Office and in other countries.

www.eHarlequin.com

Printed in U.S.A.

ABOUT THE AUTHOR

Lisa spends her days writing the dreams playing in her head. Before becoming a writer, Lisa lived the life of a corporate executive, often taking the red-eye flight out of town and flying home for the excitement of a Little League baseball game. Visit Lisa at www.lisareneejones.com.

Books by Lisa Renee Jones

HARLEQUIN BLAZE
339—HARD AND FAST
442—LONE STAR SURRENDER
559—HOT TARGET

HARLEQUIN NOCTURNE
THE BEAST WITHIN
BEAST OF DESIRE
BEAST OF DARKNESS

Special thanks to Casey and Ethan Maxwell for helping with my military research. Janice, once again, for proofing and proofing and proofing again while living the deadlines with me. And Diego—for driving the U-Haul from NY to Colorado so I could write this trilogy.

Prologue

QUICKSAND. That was what you called a mission that went from bad to worse with every maneuver you made.

Sergeant Bobby Evans sat inside a C-130 Hercules awaiting takeoff from the U.S. aircraft carrier *Vincent* with four of the twelve soldiers in his Special Ops team, "Crazy Aces." It was a name they'd come by honestly, doing crazy things like today's HALO, a high-altitude low-opening jump from thirty thousand feet. The mission was to extract the ten-year-old son of the newly elected American ally, Iraqi president Aban Kaleb Sadr, from Al Qaeda hostiles.

Free-falling at high altitudes came with risks, from unconsciousness to frostbite, but was necessary to stay off enemy radar. A HALO was a death-defying act that could give even veterans like the Aces a sense of quicksand, he supposed. But in seven years of Special Ops duty, and more than his share of HALOs, Bobby had seen quicksand only three times while a mission played out—and every one of those three times had been a bloodbath he'd have nightmares about the rest of his life.

Sitting next to Bobby, Mike Reynolds, the youngest of the Aces at twenty-eight, pulled out a picture of his fiancée, Jennifer, from beneath his jump jacket. "This is it, the last time I'm going to watch out for your sorry Texan asses," he scoffed, referring to the roots that Bobby shared with Caleb Martin and "Cowboy" Ryan Walker, the two other Aces along for this ride with them. "I'm going home to damn good New York pizza and a hot woman. Adios muchachos."

Both Bobby and Mike were up for reenlistment, and Bobby had no idea why he hadn't signed, sealed and delivered his new contract. But Mike, lovesick puppy that he was, had already opted out. He was gone in two weeks and none of the Aces were complaining, but not because they didn't love the guy like a blood brother—because they did. The Aces were tight. Family without the ancestry. But ever since Mike had met Jennifer six months ago on leave, he'd been operating with the wrong head in control.

And Bobby understood. He used to have his own Jennifer back home twisting his gut in knots. The irony of the shared name didn't sit well with Bobby one bit. Not when his Jennifer had been, and always would be, the love of his life. The woman he would never forget, could never completely let go. The fact that a mutual, close friend's upcoming wedding was stirring old feelings only brought that fact closer to light. He'd never stopped checking on his old flame, keeping up with her from a distance, but seeing her up-close and personal, facing what he'd left behind, wasn't going to be easy.

"Put the flipping picture away and focus," Bobby said sourly, that quicksand feeling sliding from his feet to his knees and threatening to climb. "I don't want to ship you back to your woman in a body bag."

Caleb sat beside Ryan, directly across from Bobby and Mike, his head against the wall, eyes shut. "I'd rather jump without a chute than be led around by my dick like you are," he mumbled, lifting his head and casting Mike a damning, icy-blue look.

"You're a dick," Mike grumbled roughly, stuffing the picture back in his jacket.

"A happy-to-reenlist-and-be-single dick, at that," Caleb agreed.

The engine roared to life, and Bobby flipped his headset on. The heavy thrum of engines filled the next twenty minutes until a buzzer sounded the ten-minute warning. Instantly all the men were on their feet, adjusting their equipment and preparing the oxygen masks they'd wear for their jump.

Ryan, Bobby's closest friend, made his customary announcement in his headset. "Let's go get 'crazy,' Aces." His gaze shifted to Mike, as he added, "Soon you can be pussy-whipped all day and all night, and nobody but your woman is going to give you a hard time."

Laughter erupted in Bobby's ears, but there was a subtle tension lacing the air, and Bobby and Ryan shared a look. He felt the quicksand, too.

At the five-minute buzzer, all masks were in place and the doors slid open. Headsets were turned off. This would be a silent jump. They were ghosts, off radar, nonexistent to even their own government. All hands latched on to the rail on the ceiling as a wicked wind screamed a warning and then pounded against them with the force of being hit with a concrete slab.

The jump conditions were far from favorable, but

neither were the Iraqi boy's chances of making it through the night. At the one-minute buzzer, there was a final check of oxygen tanks and chutes in preparation for a jump that would end in a low chute pull that left no time for a backup if anything went wrong.

At exactly 0100, with the night as their cover, and a few mountainsides in view, Caleb saluted and exited the plane in a headfirst free fall. Ryan followed. As Mike started forward, Bobby shackled the younger Ace's arm, for reasons he couldn't explain. Instinct. Warning. He didn't know. Bobby checked his chute. Then pointed to Mike's chest and then his own before twisting two fingers together, telling him silently he would have his back.

Mike gave a nod, all jesting gone at this point. They did their jobs. They knew the risks and they took them seriously. The first few seconds of the jump were critical. The jumper had to claim control from the wind and find body position.

Mike jumped, and never got the chance at control. The wind gusted, smashing him against the plane. Suddenly, Mike was spiraling downward, his body out of position. Mike made no attempt at correction. He was either unconscious or paralyzed with panic. Either way, if Mike didn't or couldn't pull his chute, he'd be dead. There was no auto-pull for a HALO.

Bobby jumped after him, adrenaline rocketing through him, as he forced himself into the cool-under-fire mentality that would be a necessity if both he and Mike were going to survive this.

The wind beat at Bobby, but he worked through it, forced his position, and sent himself into a purposeful spiral. In twenty seconds, he came level with Mike and wrapped himself around him with a jolting collision of bodies. Mike didn't react. He was out and Bobby didn't have time to check for a pulse. They were thirty seconds from pull, which was only twelve hundred feet before the ground, and Bobby's heart was thundering like that plane engine. One chute wouldn't hold them both. He had to pull Mike's and get away fast enough to pull his own. A near impossibility.

Struggling, Bobby tried to right their body positions, but Mike was dead weight. Somehow, he found a feet-first position, when Mike suddenly jerked and came awake, his eyes meeting Bobby's. Bobby breathed a sigh of relief, as he shoved away from Mike. He had pulled his chute and was under canopy in seconds and so was Mike. But that quicksand kept coming.

Gunfire splattered across the terrain as Bobby's feet hit the ground, and he instantly separated himself from his chute, dumped his oxygen tank and mask, dropping low to the ground. Mike was facedown and unmoving a foot away, and Bobby silently cursed. More gunfire chattered a deadly song nearby. Blessed returning fire followed. Ryan and Caleb were ground level, and they had his back.

Their landing zone positioned the Aces three kilometers from the enemy's camp, which sat nestled inside a mountain range, and that enemy now knew they were here. So much for a surprise attack, but they would improvise. The Aces always did. If Sadr's son was alive, they'd get him out of here.

Surrounded by mountains that could easily conceal shooters, Bobby felt like a sitting duck. He scrambled toward Mike. That twist of dread he'd felt in the plane returned, now more like a sharp slice of a knife.

Quickly, Bobby detached Mike's equipment, going cold in the hot night as stickiness brushed his fingers. He kept moving. Mike would survive. He'd make him survive.

His best option was dragging Mike, staying low, though carrying him would be faster. It would also make them one big bull's-eye target. Bobby started moving and gained assistance from Ryan. Caleb took up a position above them, holding off the enemy the best he could.

They were under heavy fire by the time Bobby and Ryan had Mike hidden behind the steep rock of the towering mountainside they'd landed nearby. Flipping him over, Ryan shined a light on Mike. Blood seeped from a cut in his head and a bullet wound in his upper chest. That quicksand that had been waiting for Bobby swallowed them up right then and there. He held his breath and felt for a pulse. Relief washed over him as he found a weak one. Mike wasn't dead…yet. There was no help until extraction. Bobby made fast work of tying off the wound the best he could, with the limited medic supplies in his vest. When he was done, Bobby's and Ryan's eyes collided through the shadowy night as they united in the only emotion they could afford in the middle of enemy territory. Anger over Mike's injuries. That he might die when he was about to go home for good. He couldn't die. And both of them wanted some Al Qaeda ass and they wanted it now.

Suddenly Caleb appeared, sliding down the mountainside, machine gun in hand, gunfire echoing in the funnel of sweltering August heat. "We have to move! Now!" He looked at Mike and cursed.

"Go!" Bobby ordered Ryan. "Get out of here!"

Ryan hesitated only a split second before he was in action, already firing his weapon. Bobby dragged Mike to a dark corner, under a ledge where he'd leave him until backup arrived, though it was killing him to think about walking away, if only for a brief time.

Task completed, Bobby reached inside Mike's flight suit and grabbed the picture of Jennifer, shoving it into his pocket. "I'll tell her what a lovesick pup you were, Mike," he vowed, just in case the unthinkable happened, and Mike didn't make it, an idea that instantly soured his stomach, delivering a hard revelation. Bobby knew why he hadn't signed those reenlistment papers. This wasn't the life you asked any woman to endure, not fairly. And Mike wasn't the only one with someone back home.

Bobby pushed to his feet and drew his weapons, re-solve forming. The sooner he completed this mission, the more chance Mike had of survival. Mike wouldn't die and this mission wouldn't be for nothing. The Aces were going to rescue that captive little boy and return him home safely, Mike along with him. And then Bobby had a Jennifer of his own to go see.

1

"BOBBY'S COMING into town for the wedding."

Jennifer Jones's frothy, ruby-red daiquiri froze an inch from her lips, as she blinked at the bartender, her best friend, Marcie Allen, the red-haired, feisty bride-to-be herself. An onslaught of nerves assaulted her stomach as that name "Bobby" sliced through the air of the Tavern—the Austin, Texas, bar Marcie's fiancé owned. The painful taunt had her heart drumming like a rock concert in her ears and a lock of blond hair floated across her face, appropriately mimicking the disarray that Bobby had left her heart in seven years ago.

He'd enlisted in the Army and shipped off without so much as a word of real explanation. Left her with nothing but a Dr. Jen letter. Oh, good grief. *Dear* Jen. "Joining Army. Better this way. Be happy." Nothing else. Not even an "I love you." Just thinking about the man scrambled her brain cells. Even her parents had been devastated over the loss of Bobby. They'd loved him like a son. Jennifer *had* loved him. Had, she reminded herself.

Jennifer set the drink down on the marble-slabbed

bar that separated her from Marcie, but not without a loud clunk that slopped the icy concoction over the sides. "What did you say?" she managed in a froglike croak, sickly and pathetic.

Marcie simply stood there, looking pale and kind of pathetically like Jennifer's croak moments before. Willie Nelson filled in for her, singing some sad Texas song that added insult to injury after the bad joke. Right. Bad joke! Nervous laughter bubbled from Jennifer's throat, and she picked up her drink again.

Marcie was a great many things. A true friend, proven from the day they'd met at age eleven, twenty years ago on the school bus. Jennifer had tripped and busted her lip in front of the hottest guy at Burnet Junior High. The hottie had bubbled over with loud laughter, and the crowd had joined in. Marcie to the rescue, she'd smack-talked the jerk into shame, and turned the joke on him. Yes. Marcie was a friend. What Marcie was not…was funny. She'd never had that comedic timing thing so many people had.

"Bad joke, Marcie," she said, so relieved she couldn't even be angry. She'd kill Marcie after she finished her rare, but much-needed, alcoholic beverage. She sipped delicately before adding, "And this is not the way to get me into that lime-green dress you want me to wear."

Marcie's hazel eyes glistened with trepidation. Recognizing the source of that trepidation as having nothing to do with her comment about the dress, and everything to do with Bobby, dread twisted in Jennifer's stomach.

"Please," Jennifer said, her hand shaking as she set the drink down again. "Tell me you're joking. Tell me Bobby is not coming to the wedding." Just his name

seemed to vibrate through every one of her five foot
five inches.

"I wouldn't joke about Bobby," Marcie said, suddenly
not only finding her voice, but her feisty redheaded attitude. "And the dress isn't lime. It's yellow-green, the
color of communicative healing in meditation, which
is how I want my relationship to be and why I'm happy
Bobby is coming. You need to heal. To deal with Bobby
once and for all."

Emotions assailed Jennifer, a whirlwind of memories
wrapped in prickly thorn-covered roses. "I do not need
to heal!" She'd moved on seven years ago when Bobby
had. She'd followed her dream, gone to vet school, and
opened a small Hill Country office, albeit settling for
a condo, not the cottage by Lake Travis she and Bobby
had wanted. Instead her parents had sold their pet shop
franchise and bought a lake house. Which she visited.
Which was enough. She *liked* her condo. She liked her
life.

"You don't even date," Marcie said.

"I date!" Okay. Not recently. But a girl could only
take so many *Nightmare on Elm Street,* bad nights out.
She pursed her lips, allowing anger and indignation to
wipe away the Bobby memories blasting through her
brain. "I can't believe he has the nerve to show up here
after being gone for all this time." She paused for a
heartbeat, and made an irritated sound. "Like he gives
a damn or something."

"He does care," Marcie said. "I need you to know
I've been communicating with him."

Marcie might as well have dropped a sledgeham-
mer on the bar because that admission shook Jennifer
so deeply it darn near rattled her teeth. "You've been

communicating with Bobby and didn't tell me." It wasn't even a question. It was stunned disbelief.

The "feist" in Marcie's feisty faded. "Yes," she said softly.

"How long?"

"Several years now," Marcie said, dropping her bombshell.

Had her heart stopped beating? Had the room gone utterly silent? "For several years?"

"He does care," Marcie repeated. And then, softening her voice, she added, "He worries about you."

Jennifer stared at her. Then she looked away, arms folding in front of her, memories refusing to be shoved away. Even after all these years, she could remember their first kiss as if it was yesterday. Bobby had moved from San Antonio, and like herself, was attending the University of Texas in Austin, or they might never have met. They'd met on the university campus—Jennifer walking her golden retriever, Bobby walking his German shepherd. The dogs had become fast friends; she and Bobby had become fast lovers. Her fingers raised to her mouth, remembering their first kiss, then dropped with that bittersweet memory.

The sound of snapping pulled her out of her reverie. "Hello?" Marcie said, fingers in front of her face.

Shaking herself mentally, Jennifer refocused on Marcie. Bobby had become like a big brother to Marcie; they were close. Of course they talked. Jennifer didn't want to be selfish—that Marcie felt she had to hide her relationship with Bobby said she had been.

"I'm sorry," Jennifer said, meaning it. "This is your wedding and if you want him here, you deserve to have him here. And I'll wear the yellow-green dress with a smile." *Just don't press me to deal with Bobby,* she pleaded silently.

Marcie seemed to read between the lines, a look of understanding sliding across her face. "Thank you, Jen," she murmured.

Reaching across the bar, Jen squeezed Marcie's arm and plastered on a bright smile that didn't quite make it to her eyes. "Two short weeks and you'll be a married woman."

Marcie all but glowed as she glanced across the crowded room to where Mark Snyder, her fiancé, chatted with a table of customers. Mark and Marcie, the two M's, often joked about. The two lovers. "Yeah," Marcie said in the midst of a dreamy sigh.

Mark looked up as if he felt Marcie's eyes on him and then motioned for her to join him. Obediently, Marcie darted from behind the bar. Jennifer sighed in relief, happy to have a few minutes alone.

Grabbing her purse, she decided she'd go freshen up. A little mascara, a dab of powder, and she would have a new mind-set. Her plan intact, she swiveled around on the bar stool and started to slide off.

The minute her feet hit the wood floor, she was stopped dead in her tracks as she crashed into a rock-hard chest. She stood stunned for a long moment as strong hands, familiar and warm, settled on her arms and sent an electric charge pinging around inside her, awareness instant, hot. Her body knew what her mind desperately burned to reject. Bobby Evans was standing in front of her. Touching her. The scent of him, rawly male, intensely masculine, and so damn arousing, insinuated into her senses. Seeped through to her bones.

Slowly, her eyes traveled upward, taking in his

towering six-foot-three frame—first sliding over denim-clad hips, then a soft black tee, a broad defined chest and finally his longish, fair hair that framed intense blue eyes. Those eyes now connected with hers. The impact was nothing shy of a head-on, steam-engine collision. Hot and hard. Just like his body and their sex life.

He was older now, a man fully developed and now thirty. Time had served him well; he was bigger, broader and even more appealing than before—tanned with fine lines around his eyes that spoke of experience, depth. And a life she hadn't been a part of.

"Hey, Jen." His voice was a deep baritone; his tone, intimate. Familiar. The same tone he'd used when he'd whispered naughty things in her ear during lovemaking.

She swallowed a sudden tickle in her throat. The things she had done with Bobby were, well...beyond pleasure. They were downright delicious. The man had a way of stripping away inhibitions and leaving nothing but the two of them, alone in the world. But that was then, and this was now.

"Bobby?" she asked, as if she were surprised. Well, she was, actually—surprised, that was. Which was something she'd be taking up with Marcie, wedding or not.

"You look good, Jen," he said, in an embarrassing reminder that she had on her softest, most worn Levi's and a pink T-shirt that said *I love my cat,* and that was about it. No jewelry. Not even fancy shoes.

It was that kind of day. A Thursday she wouldn't soon forget. She'd put down a dog that morning, one she'd treated for years, and watched the owner bawl like a baby. Exactly why she'd been anticipating this daiquiri and some laughs. But she'd made it through that, and she would make it through seeing Bobby again.

Marcie was right. She needed to heal. She needed to put Bobby behind her, once and for all. New beginnings were upon them. Jennifer straightened.

"You do, too," she said, managing a cool edge to her tone despite the tiny quaver, not quite suppressed. His hands still rested on her arms, making her skin tingle. She would have stepped away from him, but the bar stool was behind her and, besides, she wasn't going to run. Or hide. Or let him believe she couldn't deal with him being around her. She was an adult. She could deal. Casually, she added, "I'm surprised you're here so soon. I thought you would arrive closer to the wedding." The big day was a full two weeks away.

"Better early than late," he said, his hands dropping from her arms, leaving goose bumps in their wake. He offered nothing more in his answer, and she asked nothing more in return. They just stood there. Staring at one another. Close. Too close.

What did he see when he stared at her? Was she what he remembered? More? Less? She told herself that what he saw mattered about as much as the peanuts on the counter. A lie she swore to make truth. But his gaze slipped to her lips, and she knew he was thinking about kissing her. She was thinking about kissing him, too, and hated herself for that weakness. It would be so easy to lean in close to him, to lift to her toes, to see if their kiss still tasted of wildfire and passion. The temptation rippled through her with such demand, she wanted to scream. And yes—run.

That was not what a grown, respectable, confident

woman did. Not obviously, at least. Since running wasn't an immediate option…

Delicately, she cleared her throat. "How long will you be here?" Inwardly, she cringed. Why had she asked him that? And why was she searching his expression for a hint of his reaction to both her question, and to seeing her again?

And she found what she was looking for. There was a familiar intimacy in his gaze that touched her heart and her body. There was warmth to their nearness, a subtle sizzle, forcefully demanding her acceptance.

His brow inched up slowly. "Were you asking because you want to know how long until I leave, Jen?" He paused a split second. "Or because you want to know how long I'm staying?"

She knew what he was asking. Was she glad to see him? Yes. No. She didn't want to be, but she was. She didn't want to feel like that. Her life was fine without him. She'd spent far too long asking why he'd left. Now she simply wanted him to go away. Again.

Marcie's scream saved Jennifer from responding. "Bobby!" she yelled as she launched herself at him. Within seconds, she was giving him a bear hug.

Jennifer knew opportunity when she saw it. She ran. Darted toward the restroom. The one stall was thankfully vacant, and Jennifer quickly dashed inside, shut the door and slid the lock into place with a firm twist of her wrist.

Bobby had never been one to allow a girl her privacy. When he wanted to fight, he wanted to fight. When he wanted to talk, he wanted to talk. Even when she didn't. Well, they just made love until she did.

That thought sent a rush of heat spreading through

her limbs, and her hands shifted to her arms where he'd touched her, branded her. After all these years, she still wanted him. She wasn't sure whom she was more angry with. Marcie for giving her all of three minutes of warning that Bobby was about to show up or Bobby for making her all hot and bothered after leaving her heartbroken.

"Neither," she whispered into the wood-paneled restroom. She was ticked at herself for allowing Bobby to be such a big deal. He'd done her wrong, and she deserved better than him. It didn't matter that he was long, strong and packed with sex appeal. It didn't matter that old feelings had rushed over her upon hearing he would be attending the wedding. What mattered was what he had done to her and what she would not allow him to do again—hurt her. Right.

She was going back out there to show him she was not affected one way or the other by his presence, and darn it, it was going to be true. Okay. Maybe not true tonight, but at some point in the very near future it would be. For now, she'd settle for pretending.

Jennifer turned to exit and hesitated. Maybe she'd dab on a bit of makeup. Not because she wanted to impress him, but darn it, looking good was revenge in itself. Having him show up when she was looking beaten, broken and makeup-less was not helping with the confident, I-am-so-over-you attitude she hoped to convey.

She stepped to the mirror and tried not to cringe at the sight she'd made for Bobby. Hair in disarray, face and lips pale. She reached for her purse and then realized that if she returned to the bar with even one peep more of color, he'd decide it was on his behalf. And it would be.

Pursing her lips, she forced herself to let her purse drop back to her side. But the more she looked in that mirror, the more her hand itched to grab a tube of lipstick and some blush. She reasoned with herself. Looking like crap was better than being the stunning ex he'd lost out on. It would be her way of saying that he wasn't worthy of a fuss. Right. She so hated this plan. But she was sticking with it. She turned away from the mirror.

Sooner or later she had to go back into the bar, and face Bobby. Better now than later so she could make her excuses and go home. Alone. And then allow herself one night of self-pity, perhaps a big bubble bath. Then, eat chocolate. Lots and lots of chocolate.

Yep, that was the plan. And it was a great one until she pulled open the door to find Bobby standing in the tiny, private hallway, waiting for her.

2

TALL, BLOND AND GORGEOUS, Bobby was a dominating presence in any room, let alone the tiny hallway outside the restroom with only a nearby stairwell up as her escape. And his eyes, crystal-blue with little specks of yellow, were downright spellbinding. Especially when they pinned her in an intimate inspection that said he remembered every last inch of her and was picturing those inches right here and now. It was…arousing. It made her head spin and her heart race. Yet, still he wore that unaffected, cool, in-control edge that had always been Bobby, and had obviously grown more frustratingly sexy with time and maturity.

"Your hair is longer," he said. It had been to her chin when he'd left. It was to her shoulders now. "I like it."

That observation upset her on some level she didn't try to understand. Perhaps it was because he assumed he had a right to like or dislike anything about her life in the here and now. Or because of the fluff of his comment, addressing nothing but yet accentuating everything.

"Don't," she said flatly, wishing she couldn't smell

the spicy male scent that was so Bobby, filled with memories of hot nights and playful mornings. "Don't do the small talk and compliments. You're here. I'm here. Happy wedding to Marcie, and please let me out of this hallway."

His eyes, those damn crystal-blue eyes, studied her all too attentively, heating her inside out. He didn't immediately speak. Didn't move. Or did he? A sway forward. Yes. If anything she felt as if he'd come closer. The tiny hallway shrank, if that were even possible, and judging from the claustrophobic, trapped feeling making her heart thunder in her chest, it was.

"We should talk," he finally said in that deep voice he'd once used to whisper wicked promises in far too many public places. Like this one.

"Look, Bobby," she said, grabbing the frame of the door to steady herself. The solid door behind her reminded her how locked into this up-close-and-personal encounter with Bobby she really was. "I know you want to smooth things over between us for Marcie's sake. Done. Smooth. Nothing else to talk about. Welcome home. You look good. You like my hair. Great. See you at the rehearsal dinner."

His expression didn't change, nor did his body position, which remained close and radiating heat. "Just like that? The past is behind us?"

"Right," she agreed, trying to smile but failing miserably with a weak attempt that was more a twist of her lips. "Behind us and all is well."

His hand went to the frame above her head, and this time there was no question that he was removing the space between them. Mere inches separated them and she could barely breathe. "Then you shouldn't have any problem coming upstairs and having a drink with me," he suggested. "For old times' sake."

Jennifer's mind was spinning. She'd lost a dog today. Then found out her best friend, whom she didn't believe would ever deceive her, had been secretly conspiring with Bobby. This had been an emotional, confusing day, that clearly wasn't over yet. Because now, standing in front of her was not only the man who had secretly always held her heart, despite breaking it, but also the man she'd lain awake worried for, many a night. Fearful of the day she'd hear Bobby had died on some Army mission.

"No," she said firmly, her hand coming up and, Lord help her, almost resting on his chest. "I don't want to do this, Bobby."

He caught her hand and electricity shot up her arm. "Do what, Jen?" he asked, and then settled her hand to that delicious wall of muscled chest. "And you can touch me, Jen. I never bite unless you want me to. You know that."

This time she did willingly touch his chest, shoving him away. "Damn you, Bobby Evans. I don't know what you're trying to prove. I don't want to touch you. I don't want you to bite me or not bite me, or tell me my hair looks good. You left. Fine. But there is nothing between us now, and I won't be your local bedroom pit stop while you're here." She steeled her spine. "Now. Let me by so I can go home before I…" *Do something embarrassing and cry.* Her eyes prickled and that made her mad. She shoved his chest again. "Let me by."

He released her hand but he didn't move; he ran a hand through his hair. "Listen, Jennifer. This isn't how I planned this." There was something akin to real, raw emotion in his eyes now, all that coolness gone. And she knew she had to get out of here, before she did something foolish and asked exactly how or why he'd planned anything with her.

"Let me by, Bobby," she repeated, her voice low, calmer than she felt. Way calmer than she felt. And to her total utter relief and displeasure, he did.

BOBBY HAD TAKEN his share of blows over the years, most of which had come from U.S. enemies. A few from his Army buds during drunken altercations. Being the sober guy who didn't want to turn into his drunk father, in the middle of a bunch of drunks, turned into a bucket of laughs or a gutter of irritation. Sometimes both got the best of a guy. But being rejected by Jennifer hit him harder than any combination of those blows—like a Mack truck head-on.

He had a lot of explaining to do, including why the night before he'd enlisted pushed him over the edge, convinced him he was his father's son and would one day become his father. Bobby doubted anything he could say would easily convince Jennifer he'd left because he loved her, to protect her. But the night he'd gone…it had been a bad night that had grabbed him by the throat and held on for years to come. Still did if he was honest.

Bobby dragged himself up the stairs, a beaten dog with his tail between his legs, only to find Marcie standing at the top, hands on her hips. "Bobby! Why didn't you tell me you were coming tonight?"

"And here I thought the hug meant you were glad to see me," he said dryly, stopping midway to the top, once they were eye level.

"I am," she replied, sounding not the least bit convincing. "But your timing majorly stinks. Tonight, I told Jennifer you were coming to the wedding, and then a few minutes later, of all times, you pay a surprise early visit. Do you know how that makes me look?" He would have answered, but she didn't give him the chance. "She thinks I planned this. She thinks I knew you were coming tonight and I didn't warn her. She's completely ticked at both of us, at me. She's not supposed to be ticked at me, Bobby. She's my maid of honor."

Nothing like kicking a dog while he was down. "I know," he said and then vowed, "I'll fix it."

"Eventually," she agreed. "But I don't have time for eventually, Bobby. My wedding is in two weeks." She pressed her fingers to her temple. "Jeez. It's Wednesday, Bobby. The combo bachelor/bachelorette party is Friday night and not only is Jennifer helping me set up, but now you're also here. Look, if Jennifer shuts me out, it'll tear me apart. You have to find a way to fix this right now." She shook her head, crossed her arms in front of her chest. Her voice cracked as if she might cry. "She wouldn't even look at me when she stormed toward the door."

"I'll go see her," he said quickly. "Once I explain—"

"Don't." Marcie held up a hand and added quickly, "Not yet."

"You said now, not later," he reminded her, more than eager to charge after Jennifer. Damn it, letting her walk away had been hell. An excuse to see her again suited him fine.

"I know what I said," Marcie fumed. "But not tonight. In case you forgot in your seven years away, she never responds well without some space to process. Let me call her and explain everything. *Then* you go see her. Let her sleep on this."

"*This* meaning me."

"Yes, you!" she said. "You broke her heart."

"I didn't mean to."

"But you did and now that you're back she needs some space. That's the way she deals with things."

He remembered. He remembered everything about Jennifer; it had taken mere seconds once he'd seen her again.

"Bobby," Marcie warned. "Whatever you're thinking, stop. Please. Wait and let me talk to her."

Seven years had been far too long to wait, Bobby thought, his mind tracking back to the gut-wrenching three days when Mike had been in ICU. Life was precious and short. When Mike had pulled through, he'd had his fiancée waiting for him. His Jennifer. Bobby had come for his.

"You have until tomorrow morning," he conceded. "Then I'm going after her." He walked up the stairs and didn't give her time to argue, knowing full well she would.

Tonight, seeing Jennifer again, he knew the past and present were still one and the same. He'd been raised by a single drunk father, and one dark night, he'd let that father convince him he would be the same one day, that he'd destroy Jennifer's life as his father had tried to do his. But that was then and this was now and it was clear neither he nor Jennifer had fully put their relationship behind them. And he wasn't going to screw up and run from the future as he had the past. Nor was he giving Jennifer time to either. He had to know what could have been—and he knew now, she did, too. Even if she wasn't willing to admit that fact…yet.

WITH A GRUMBLE, Jennifer hit the snooze button on the alarm clock. She glanced at the digital display in confirmation of the early hour, six-thirty, and grumbled again before shoving aside the blankets. She had to be at her vet clinic by eight-thirty to open at nine. Usually she'd snooze a little longer, but she saw no point in trying. Not after yesterday, a day where she'd endured the tragedy of putting down a beloved pooch, followed by a visit from the man who'd been the most important relationship of her life.

Suddenly, a furry, big-eared kitty was on top of her, purring with demand. "I know, Julie. You want your special morning food." Jennifer ran her hand over the kitty's fur, though at one year old, she was hardly a kitten anymore. A big, pampered baby was more like it.

She hugged her friendly pet. The two J's. Jennifer and sweet kitty, Julie. Them against the world, and Jennifer was okay with that. Right. Okay. With. That. No Bobby. Mark and Marcie, the two M's, slid into her mind.

With a sigh, Jennifer set Julie on the floor. Julie gave her a demanding meow, followed by several more, as in ready for that food—now. "Well," she murmured, "you do have demanding down well."

Julie meowed louder, as if proving that point.

Sternly, playfully, Jennifer warned, "Wait, you little fur ball!" She quickly reset her alarm, and snatched her cell phone from the nightstand. Reluctantly, she turned it back on.

Marcie had called a good half-dozen times last night but Jennifer had nothing to say to Marcie. Not now. Not until she cooled off. Obviously Marcie thought her up-coming wedding gave her the right to do whatever she wanted. To some extent that was true, but within limits. And Bobby hit every limit Jennifer owned. Of course, with the party tomorrow night, she'd have to face her sometime then, but that gave her a day with her work to get past any remaining hurt feelings.

Jennifer shoved her feet into hot-pink slippers, glad for a small smile Julie produced as she attacked one of them. Jennifer grabbed her hot-pink, knee-length robe, a shade lighter than her cotton boxers and tank top, and slipped it over her shoulders.

She didn't do lack of sleep well, but when she was forced to, she did cranky exceptionally well. In fact, she could almost feel the crankiness rolling off her in big, powerful waves. Easier to deal with than the emotion beneath it, the ache of facing Bobby, and realizing, despite all he'd done to her, she still reacted to him. Still wanted him. She quickly brushed her teeth and considered the shower.

"Coffee," she murmured, heading to the navy-blue, rectangular-shaped kitchen. Its shiny compact prettiness had sold her on the condo, despite her lack of skill in the cooking department. She eyed the dishes in the sink she'd forgotten the night before. "Lots of coffee. I'm going to need lots of coffee." Thank goodness, despite sleep deprivation, she would have her animals to keep her busy and force more smiles today.

And on that note, Jennifer put the meowing kitty out of her misery, and filled her food bowl. Next, she snagged the coffeepot and headed to the sink.

Holding it under the water, Jennifer froze when a knock sounded on her front door.

Jennifer set the pot down on the counter and turned off the water, the thundering of her heart exploding in her ears. Another knock and she steeled herself to answer the door. She pulled the sash to her robe into place and tied it a bit more firmly than necessary. As if a cotton tie would somehow protect her from what— correction, *who*—was waiting for her on the other side of that door. She could do this. She could face Bobby and be strong. She was strong. She was happy. Bobby showing up didn't change anything.

And because she was a smart girl, who'd lived alone her entire adult life, she did the smart thing, not to mention the thing that gave her a chance to stall, but that was beside the point—she called out rather than opened the door. "Who is it?"

"Man bearing gifts," came the all-too-familiar voice, all-too-richly buttered with memories and heat. The kind of heat only one man had ever conjured in her. That he still got to her, that he stroked her into arousal so effortlessly, with a simple spoken word filled with memories, agitated her almost as much as the idea of a gift. Did he really think a present would erase seven years of silence?

"Go away, Bobby," she said, her voice irritatingly raspy with uncontained emotion. "Whatever it is, I don't want it."

"You want this," he assured her. "I guarantee it."

"I don't," she said sternly. *But I want you,* she added silently, hating him for having power over her after all this time. She firmed her voice. "Go away, Bobby."

A beat of tension-laden silence followed before he replied, "Venti White Mocha, no foam, no whip, extrahot."

Her eyes went wide, jaw slack. The nerve of him to bring her favorite drink, to use the past against her. This was manipulation, and it was wrong.

Jennifer forgot the robe, the hair sticking up, the lack of makeup. Forgot the hidden fear of facing Bobby again and somehow shattering into the emotional wreck she'd promised herself she was not. She yanked open the door, fully intending a verbal attack and falling flat on her proverbial face the moment she brought Bobby into focus.

He stood there, a mere few feet away, dangerously sexy. Denim clad—God, how the man made denim look delicious—light blond stubble shading his jaw, crystal-blue eyes twinkling with awareness and mischief, holding a Venti Starbucks, a box of her favorite donuts and, damn it, her heart. He still had her heart. And she knew, in that moment, he'd had it for far too long. He didn't deserve it. Not after the way he'd left her.

His coming home for the wedding was a good thing. Good because now she could face him and get over him. Now, she could take back her heart, once and for all.

3

HOT ON THE SPOT. That was Bobby when Jennifer opened her door in her skimpy robe, displaying miles of leg and sexy, slender curves. In fact, he was so hot, the Texas sun might as well have been at high noon—because he sure was. Hot. Hard. Aching with need well beyond the physical. With memories of Jennifer waking up in his arms, in his life.

"Peace offering," he explained, indicating the coffee and the box of chocolate-covered Krispy Kremes she so adored. "For showing up unexpectedly last night. I have jelly-filled in the car for Marcie. She's pretty upset at me for getting her in trouble with you and she's still letting me stay at her place. She didn't know I was coming into town early, Jen."

She bit her lip, the full bottom one he'd like to bite himself. Oh, yeah. He remembered nipping that lip, then softly licking it. His gaze lingered on her mouth, then on the slow rise and fall of her chest.

"This isn't going to work," she said flatly.

His gaze lifted to the stubborn set of her jaw, the one telling him how desperately she was clinging to resolve to keep him at a distance. Translation. This *was* working.

He offered her a gentle smile and a verbal nudge. "Oh, come on, Jen," he urged. "Let me in."

She gave him a dubious look, and finally said, "Letting you in my door means I want the coffee and donuts. Nothing more."

Yes. That was yes. "Understood," he agreed, stepping forward before she could change her mind, with every intention of making this morning about far more than coffee and donuts.

Crowding the doorway, he forced her to either accept his nearness or back away. As predicted, she backed away, but not before his nostrils flared with her soft, floral scent, laced with jasmine. A scent he'd imagined a million times over the past seven years.

Once he was in the hallway, Bobby resisted the urge to turn to her. She was close, so close. But even if his hands weren't full, reaching for her now, no matter how tempting, would be premature, a mistake sure to backfire. The time for that would come—sooner rather than later.

For now, he charged forward, down a short hallway, determined to reach deeper into her life, starting with the intimacy of being inside the place she called home. He wanted to know what her life had become, what she had become. Besides being more beautiful than ever, even at this early hour.

"Bobby!" she objected from behind him, a moment before the door slammed shut. "You can't just barge in like this," Jennifer said, sounding a bit breathless and a lot sexy, as she caught up to him. "We can eat the donuts at the kitchen bar."

Bobby sauntered down a short flight of stairs to a sunken living room with Pergo floors. His chest tightened as the cozy little room drew him in, surrounding him with rich navy blues. Jennifer loved blue. Navy mostly, but all shades. Her dorm room had been a navy blue she'd insisted was "velvet blue."

His lips twitched as he remembered kissing her and telling her that her lips were velvet soft, and then making love to her on the "velvet blue" comforter.

Bobby sat down on the overstuffed couch, placing the donuts and coffee on the table before him, and then ran his hand over the cushion. "Is this navy blue or velvet blue?"

Her eyes went wide and a pink flush touched her pale perfect skin, telling him she remembered that day on her velvet bedspread as much as he did. "Come sit with me," he urged, rescuing her from a reply.

She crossed her arms in front of her, staring at the couch, his hand and the coffee. "Why are you back, Bobby?"

Why was he back? That was a loaded question. He could say for Marcie's wedding—which was partially true—but overall, a copout, and they'd both know it. He'd never lied to Jennifer, and he wasn't going to start now. Besides, there wasn't an easy answer anyway. Aside from—he had to come. He *had* to see her. Still, too much too soon, he decided.

Instead, he simply replied, "What's wrong with old friends sharing coffee and donuts?" And then added in a soft plea, "It's getting cold."

"Old friends," she said softly. "Is that what we are?"

Their eyes locked and held, tension, both sexual and

emotional, stretching between them. "Aren't we?" he challenged. Friends and so much more.

Indecision flashed across her face. "I should go put on some clothes," she said, clearly avoiding his question.

"I won't complain if you stay in your robe," he teased gently.

The pink in her cheeks flushed redder, as if he hadn't seen her naked a million times over. "Bobby," she chided.

"Sorry," he said, meaning it. He didn't want to make her uncomfortable. But he did want her. "I couldn't resist. I promise not to look." She gave him a disbelieving gape. He lifted a defeated hand. "Okay, I won't look—much. Or I'll try not to. Really." Not really. He scrubbed his jaw in further defeat. "How about I promise not to stay long?"

She tilted her head, studied him. "I don't know if I should grab something and throw it at you or just drink the coffee and eat the donuts."

"While I'm sure throwing something at me might hold a certain degree of pleasure," he commented, "I recommend caffeine consumption before making that judgment."

"Valid point," she conceded, and walked to the other end of the couch. "For the record, I reserve the right to throw something, or many things, at you, one or more times, during the next two weeks."

He smiled. "I can live with that though your father will probably do it for you after the wedding."

"True," she agreed happily.

Her father was protective. Bobby had hurt her. He'd have some things to say to Bobby and Bobby guessed she wasn't feeling too inclined to stop him. Jennifer picked up the coffee and sipped. Her lashes fluttered, dark circles on creamy white skin as she added, "Okay. For the moment, the coffee is way better than throwing something at you."

"That's good to hear."

She blinked several times. "Thank you. I so needed this."

"That's what you used to say every morning."

She breezed past the comment. "I've never been very human without my coffee, I guess," she admitted and grabbed a donut.

"I guess some things never change," he teased, barely containing the urge to reach for her. He wanted to kiss her. To taste her. To lay her down on that couch and feel her close.

She bit her bottom lip. "Bobby—"

"You have chocolate on your mouth," he said. Taking advantage of her hands being full—one with coffee, one with a donut—he reached over and ran his finger to swipe off the offending icing, when he longed to use his tongue. He licked his finger. "Good." Her. Not the chocolate.

"Stop," she objected, setting the donut on the box and the coffee on the table. "I know what you're trying to do."

He arched a brow. "Which would be what?"

She glowered. "Bobby—"

He leaned a little closer. "I like hearing you say my name. Even when you're mad."

"I'm not mad," she said and pushed to her feet. "And I'm not having sex with you. I'm not some two-week, wedding fling."

He stopped. "Wait," he said. "We're talking about

sex, and I don't know about it? But okay on the two weeks." He lowered his voice to a velvety-blue shade. She looked adorable, all flustered and ready to take his head off. "Two weeks would never be enough."

Her eyes went wide and she opened her mouth to speak when her cell phone rang, from what sounded like the pocket of her robe. "You know it's Marcie," he said. "You should talk to her. Put her out of her misery. She thinks you're mad, too."

"I *am* mad, at *her*," she said, her brows dipping.

"She didn't know I was coming," he said.

"I know," she said.

He narrowed his gaze. "Why don't I believe you?"

"She didn't know you were going to be there last night," she said. "But for 'years,' she admitted, you two talked and I never knew." Her voice cracked, lifted. "And it shouldn't matter she was talking to you and I didn't know, but clearly Marcie was smart enough to know it *would* matter, because here I am, standing in front of you, wanting to throw something again— because *it matters*." She flung her hands in the air and let them drop. "I'm going to shower. Please don't be here when I get back."

It mattered because she cared. Which meant Bobby had two options. Let her go and give her space, as Marcie had declared was necessary. Or he could do what he would have done in the past and launch a full-out assault. Make his intentions clear.

Bobby went for the all-out assault. He was on his feet, pulling her close in seconds. And though not his intention, before he could stop himself, he was kissing her.

She gasped into his mouth and he swallowed it,

drinking her in like sweet honeyed tea on a sizzling summer day. And though she tried to resist, holding herself stiff, unyielding, the minute his tongue stroked hers, she surrendered. His hand slid up her back, molding her close, if only for a moment, when her cell phone rang again.

Bobby reached into her pocket and pulled it out, forcing himself to end the kiss. "Talk to Marcie," he said. "You're mad at me, not her. She needs you." He pressed the phone into her hand, stared down at her, and then turned and headed for the door.

"Don't come back, Bobby," she called behind him.

He paused and turned to look at her only long enough to vow, "I'm already back."

Bobby passed the kitchen, certain Jennifer wouldn't follow him to the door. Not after that flipping amazing kiss that said they could easily rekindle the bedroom bliss and a whole lot more. Jennifer would wait for him to leave, and then analyze and plan a way to deal with him. For now, Bobby had to settle for repairing her friendship with Marcie.

But tomorrow was another day. And after that kiss, he was certain, he had to have another. For the first time in seven years, there was more than a mission, and some unnamed enemy. He felt like more than a machine. He felt alive.

4

"YOU KNOW YOU STILL WANT HIM," Marcie declared.

It was near dark, hours after her encounter with Bobby, and Jennifer stood in Marcie's kitchen, stirring chocolate mousse for the next night's bachelor/bachelorette party. The two acres sprawling Lake Travis property, with the ranch-style house, that had once been Mark's parents' place, was a perfect location for such fun.

Jennifer grimaced and pointed at Marcie with the spoon. "I *do not* still want him. And I wouldn't have called you to apologize if I'd be coming over here to be abused."

Marcie reached over the counter and scooped some of the mousse off the spoon a moment before it would have dropped on the counter. She tasted it. "Hmm. Good stuff." Her eyes twinkled. "And yes. You would have apologized. Because you might be stubborn, but you're a good friend. And yes, you do still want Bobby."

Jennifer glared at her, and because she couldn't deny either of Marcie's claims anymore, she ignored them and did the only respectable thing to do under fire.

She licked the chocolate-covered spoon and had the naughty idea of licking the same chocolate off Bobby. She dropped the spoon into the sink as if it were on fire. "We need to have Mark bring in the rest of the champagne from our cars."

"So you can have *your* car back and run away from this conversation?" Marcie challenged. "Forget it." She leaned on the counter, smiling evilly. "Why don't you just have sex with Bobby and get it out of your system before the wedding? It might be easier on all of us."

"Would you stop?" Jennifer demanded, pressing her hands to her jeans-clad hips, her favorite black pair that matched her black tank top with a pink heart in the center—the jeans she had *absolutely* not picked because they made her butt look smaller than the blue ones and Bobby might show up to see said butt.

"If *you* stop avoiding," Marcie countered. "Deal with Bobby and move on." She held up a hand the second Jennifer started to speak. "And don't tell me you have, because we both know you haven't. You never got closure, Jennifer. Now you have a chance. Sleep with him, girl. If for no other reason but the satisfaction of knowing you can do it and walk away. You, not him this time. Sexual energy is very healing."

"Oh, good grief," Jennifer blurted. "Enough with the healing energy."

"Okay," Marcie said, grabbing a champagne bottle from a case sitting on the floor. "No healing energy. Let's try alcohol-induced courage. Why don't we pop one of these babies open and loosen you up?"

Jennifer pressed her hand to her face before fixing a glare on Marcie. "I don't need to loosen up, because

I told you," she said, glaring, "I'm not sleeping with Bobby."

"Ever?" At the sound of Bobby's voice behind her, Jennifer's heart stopped beating for an instant.

Her eyes met Marcie's far too amused ones and she mouthed "I'm going to kill you" before whirling around to face the inevitable—Bobby looking like sin poured into denim and cotton. "Never," she assured him, her knees weak.

And then damn him, his mouth twitched, the one she'd kissed that very morning.

"Never is a long time. I reserve the right to try to change your mind."

The declaration sent a sudden flutter of butterflies through her stomach. She wanted him to want her. Wanted to kiss him again. It scared her how much, terrified her how easily she could once again have her heart broken.

Marcie cleared her throat. "Since you're here, Bobby," she said, "can you grab Mark and get the rest of the champagne out of the cars?"

"Sure," he said. "Where are the keys?"

"Mark has mine," Marcie said. "Is your car locked, Jen?"

She nodded. "Yes," she said. "I'll get my keys." From her purse. By the door. That she couldn't get to without squeezing through the slim hallway where Bobby's big, muscular, too-sexy body currently resided. The same way he'd been in the back of her mind, blocking the way into the future. Damn. Marcie was right. She hadn't dealt with Bobby. She'd simply ignored her memories.

"They're in my purse," she said to Bobby and motioned him onward. "I'll follow you out."

He stood there an instant, his eyes lingering on her lips, as if he were thinking of the kiss they'd shared, before he stepped backward, into the hallway, and motioned her forward.

"Ladies first," he challenged, leaving her a tiny space to pass.

Bobby arched an expectant brow. It was then that Jennifer realized Marcie was right—whatever happened needed to be on her terms. Melting into the floor wasn't on her terms. She had to face Bobby and face her past. For now, though, she'd settle for getting past him and to her car.

Jennifer drew her shoulders back and charged forward, self-consciously thinking about the black jeans she'd be strutting in front of him. Wondering if he still thought she was attractive. Telling herself he did or he wouldn't have kissed her. Telling herself that it didn't matter, but knowing it most definitely did.

She breezed past Bobby with a determined stride that brought her inches from touching him, but she stared forward, refusing to look at him. Oh, but she felt him, might as well have touched him, *imagined* touching him. Her skin tingled, her stomach did a funny, fluttery thing. And his scent. Her nostrils flared with his delicious, familiar scent. All spicy and male. She knew that smell so well; she knew the name of the cologne, and the hot way it meshed with his body chemistry and turned to an aphrodisiac that drove her insane.

Jennifer grabbed her purse from the table by the door and turned to find Bobby towering over her. She swallowed hard. He was close. Inches. Awareness tingled in her nerve endings.

She was so in trouble. Clearly, avoiding Bobby wasn't

an option. Definitely. Not. But she would not have sex with Bobby either.

Holding up her keys, she jangled them. "I'll walk out with you." *And leave,* but she didn't say that.

Mark appeared in the hallway, his shoulder-length dark hair tied at his neck, a contrast to Bobby's short blond locks. And where Bobby was tall, broad and athletic, Mark was simply tall and lean.

"I've been ordered to remove all boxes from the cars," Mark said, his tone laced with a hint of irritation. He eyed Bobby and nodded. "Hey, man. Sorry I didn't say much when you came in. I was on the phone with one of our liquor vendors."

They shook hands, as if they'd just recently met. Then again, for all she knew, Bobby had been home before now, and she didn't know. Marcie had only started dating Mark two years before, but they might have casually met before now. Though Bobby's mother had died of cancer when he was in his teens, and he had no siblings, his father owned an auto shop outside San Antonio, a little over an hour away. It was hard to believe that in seven years he hadn't been home once.

"Talk Marcie into jumping yet?" Bobby asked Mark.

"No," he said. "She's too chicken. But I'm all about giving it a go. When do you have in mind?"

"Jumping?" Jennifer asked, frowning, not sure if she'd missed something.

"You are so *not* skydiving right before our wedding!" Marcie said, rushing to Mark's side, glaring up from her five-three to Mark's towering six-three. "You're a computer programmer turned bar owner, and while that shows impressive diversity, you are not Special Forces, like Bobby."

Special Forces. Jennifer had not even known Bobby was Special Forces. Her stomach twisted a little.

"Still," Mark said. "I'm going to jump while Bobby is here and can go with me. And you might as well come with us. I mean, if anything happens to me the wedding is off anyway."

Oh, ouch. Jennifer knew that wasn't going to go over well. And it didn't. "Mark!"

Jennifer and Bobby exchanged a cringe and headed to the door. Outside, the hot Texas night encased them as assuredly as the tension, both sexual and emotional.

Bobby whistled as the door shut behind them. "I wish I would never have brought up jumping last night. They've been snapping at each other ever since. Not exactly what I call wedding bliss."

"Wedding jitters," Jennifer corrected. "It's not uncommon, and it's not your fault. And they've been at it a few days now." Guilt twisted in her gut as they stopped beside her blue Mazda 626. She drew a breath and turned to face him. "Which is why I really want to put the past behind us, Bobby. The next two weeks is about them, not us. Let's call a truce."

He stared at her, his deep blue, beautiful eyes smoldering. "A truce it is," he said. "Why don't we start this truce by finding me a way out of inviting Mark to skydive. He's determined to go. She's determined he won't. Why don't you convince Marcie to come along?" He wiggled a brow. "A foursome."

Ignoring the joke, and the undercurrent of "coupleness" or whatever real word one might call it that escaped her now, Jennifer argued, "Marcie is already upset over that idea, Bobby. Pressuring her isn't going to help matters."

"Well, I can see the look in Mark's eye. He's out to prove something and this isn't over. But we can end it together, like I said. Come jump with us. Convince Marcie to come, too."

She shook her head. "Me. Jumping out of a plane? Not in this lifetime. That's way too out of control for me." She opened her door and tossed her purse inside, before clicking the lock to the back door where the champagne was stored.

"You can tandem jump with me," he said. "You'd be tied to me. I'll have control then. I'll keep you safe."

He'd have control. There lay her problem. Bobby had control—when he'd left; for the past seven years, as she'd secretly wanted, needed and wondered; and now, because she was running from him. *She* had to take control, stop wallowing in the past. Deal with the right here and now.

"You can trust me," Bobby said in a low, sandpaper-rough voice. "When I left—"

She did the only thing she knew to shut him up—she kissed him. She stepped forward, pressed her hand on the solid wall of his chest, pushed to her toes and kissed him. That was taking control. This was taking control. She was taking control.

They hadn't been in love. Love endured. Love was honest. Love didn't run away and never look back. They'd been in lust, and she was all about lust in that moment. All about pleasure. For two weeks, he was here, the man who'd been the best sex of her life. She'd be a fool to run from his flavor of pleasure. She would enjoy him, and then *she* would say goodbye.

Starting with this kiss. The instant Jennifer's mouth touched Bobby's, he pulled her closer, taking her mouth, as if he feared she might change her mind. His tongue parted her lips, intimately, full of demand. One of his hands tangled in her hair, the other slid up her back, pressing her close, molding her against all that delicious hard muscle. Her hands slid over his back. Long, strong thighs entwined with hers, his hips settling against hers. His erection, already thick, hard, pressing against her stomach.

She moaned into his mouth, heat pooling in the V of her body. She'd told herself she'd kissed him to shut him up, and while true, it had also been for pleasure. The same reason her hand was under his shirt, her palm absorbing warm, taut skin. Feeling pleasure was so much better than talking about the past. Feeling pleasure. Yes. *Pleasure.* He knew exactly where to touch her. She knew exactly where to touch him.

Images of their naked bodies entwined, their passionate, impossible-to-forget lovemaking sizzled in her mind and melted her body against his. Kissing him, tasting him, feeling him close.

"Jennifer," he murmured against her lips, pulling back to stare at her. "I—"

She pressed her fingers to his lips. "Don't talk," she said. "Kiss me again."

"Bobby!" came Marcie's shout from the door. "Some guy called the house phone. He says it's urgent."

"Damn it," Bobby cursed under his breath, closing his hand around hers and kissing it. "I'm sorry. I gave the Army an emergency number. I'm on leave but—"

"Duty first," she said, relief washing over her. "Then

fun." She'd started this game without planning. That was a lot for Jennifer.

"Bobby!" Marcie yelled again.

He stared down at her, his dark lashes narrowing around intelligent blue eyes, as if he were suspicious of what she would do next. He hesitated, then kissed her firmly. "Don't go anywhere," he ordered, steel determination in his voice. "We have to talk." And then he was half walking, half jogging to the house.

She watched him, the long, lithe way he moved—like a soldier she didn't know, but a lover she knew all too well. A past she didn't want to know at all if it wasn't between the sheets. It was easier that way. No, there would be no talking. There'd be more kissing. They'd do more pleasuring. They'd do it on her terms, though.

Tomorrow night at the party, where champagne would be plentiful, the fun and adventure would be on high octane. She closed the trunk and slid into the car, deciding the case of champagne in the car would wait until tomorrow. A smile touched her lips as she turned the ignition. There might even be some of that chocolate mousse on Bobby. A simple plan of pleasure.

What more could a girl want? Okay, bad question, one that stirred the wrong emotions. As did the idea of that phone call perhaps ordering him back to duty, perhaps without a goodbye, yet again. She dismissed the thought and put the car into gear. Refocused on her plan. On the chocolate mousse, and its removal, one delicious, sensual lick at a time. Oh, yes. Lots of licking. No talking.

THERE HAD NEVER BEEN a woman that tasted like honey, sunrise and heaven the way Jennifer did. Not before her. Not after her. Heat, desire and readiness climbed through his limbs, burned molten heat in his blood. Bobby all but ran to the door, eager to get the call over with, and return to Jennifer. The sound of tires on gravel stopped him in his tracks.

"Damn," he murmured under his breath, scrubbing his jaw, watching the car pull away. He'd had her—in his arms, kissing him freely, willing to kiss him again. And in a snap, she was gone. Kind of like he had been all those years ago. Damn again. He deserved to be worked up and left behind. He deserved anything she did to him ten times over, and he wasn't above admitting it.

Bobby fought the urge to run to the end of the driveway, to cut her off before she departed, and to tell her that and more. But when the Army called, a soldier answered, even one close to walking away from reenlistment. Especially when he knew what the call was about—the same reason he'd been working on getting out to that skydiving operation.

He'd been in town all of a few hours, when Bobby had gotten "official orders" that trumped his leave. When he'd been told to check out some ex-Special Ops guy named Rocky Smith, who Bobby didn't know from Adam, but apparently owned the skydiving operation Texas Hotzone, about thirty miles outside Austin, in the adjacent small city of San Marcus. Seemed Rocky was catching some buzz in connection to a Mexican drug lord, and the Army wanted Bobby to see what he could find out. Even on leave, he wasn't on leave. He reached the bottom of the porch stairs to find Marcie waiting for him at the top, hands on her hips. "She left with the champagne," she said. "What did you do to her?"

Bobby grimaced as he double-stepped to the top. "I didn't do anything to her," he said. But he wanted to do plenty. To kiss every last inch of her and do it all over again. And again.

Marcie gave him a skeptical look and offered him the phone. "Sergeant Walker," Bobby said into the phone. The reply was simple. Call in on a secure line at 0800. He hung up.

"That was it?" she asked. "The call is over?"

He nodded. "Report orders."

"Not now?" she asked urgently.

"The day after the wedding," he said, though he had a few more days before he was actually due to report. But by then, he would have made his decision. He was staying or he was reenlisting. "You know. You're all worked up and cranky, you're going to run Mark off before he says 'I do.'"

She opened her mouth to argue and then shut it. "I know."

"You're both nervous and excited," he said. "If the man wants to skydive, to escape that for a day, don't hold him back. Go with him."

"I don't want him to get hurt," she said.

"He won't," he said. "And neither will you. Make up with him."

"I have been kind of cranky," she conceded.

"Kind of?" he asked.

She glowered. "Don't push your luck, Bobby, because I'm still feeling real darn cranky."

He laughed. "Then be cranky. At me. Not Mark." He turned her to the door. "Go. Now. Talk to your man and whatever else you do when you make up with him. I'll see you tomorrow."

She eyed him over her shoulder. "I don't want to run you off."

"Go," he said, giving her a nudge to the door. "I'm fine. Make sure the wedding I came for takes place."

This time she didn't argue. Marcie disappeared into the house, and Bobby turned back to the driveway. He had to deal with the Army tonight, because he wasn't about to risk another interruption with Jennifer. She'd be working tomorrow. So, that left tomorrow night at the party where he had a mission.

He was glad for the interruption tonight. He'd been about to confess his sins, explain the past despite knowing the timing was wrong. He had to make her listen, pull down her guard, before he unraveled the mess that had been in his head the night he'd left, and the years of justifying that followed. That meant a lot of loving, touching and kissing. And then they were most definitely going to talk. That was his mission and Bobby never failed a mission.

Nor was he going to fail Jennifer. Not this time.

5

Friday arrived and the party was on. And so was the seduction as far as Jennifer was concerned. She might not be good at dating, in fact, some might say disastrous, but she was good at seducing Bobby. At least, the old Bobby, and she refused to consider the present-day Bobby might be seduced differently than in the past, because then her confidence would falter, and her plan with it.

Dressed in cowboy boots, slim-cut, faded blue jeans she'd bought earlier that day, and a pink formfitting, deep V-neck T-shirt accented by a Victoria's Secret bra that lifted her C cup in an intentionally enticing way, Jennifer stood on the back patio of Mark and Marcie's house. The unique blend of both bachelor and bachelorette party was in full swing.

With the nearest neighbor's house a mile away, a DJ freely spun music. At present Carrie Underwood's "Casanova Cowboy" filled the air, with about ten couples dancing on the small round dance floor in the center of the yard; moments before he'd played Aerosmith's "Walk this Way."

At least thirty people, friends and neighbors, mingled in various locales of the house, but the backyard was most definitely the hot spot, where kegs, Margarita machines, long tables of food like the one she stood next to, and barbecue grills, proved to be an enticing lure.

Jennifer sipped a glass of champagne freely, freely because, per Mark's demand, all guests had left their keys and cab fare at the door. Only the enjoyment of her drink would have been easier, if Marcie wasn't casting her a scrutinizing stare, ready to hit her with a million Bobby questions. Until now, Jennifer had avoided Marcie's inquisition. Friday clinic, then the rush to get ready for the party, had thankfully made that possible. But the buck stopped here, and she knew it.

"That kiss last night," Marcie said, turning to the table and selecting a plump strawberry. "The low-cut shirt tonight, the hot-pink lipstick…you're going to take Bobby to bed and send him packing. Aren't you?"

Jennifer glowered. "Will you please obsess about your own husband-to-be, not my man who was to be, but no longer is?"

Her brow quirked as she dipped the strawberry in chocolate. "Decided the chocolate-covered Bobby appealed, aye?"

A slow smile slid onto Jennifer's lips. "Maybe," she admitted coyly. The truth was, she'd found herself walking down memory lane. The bedroom variety. The intimate, sexy things they'd done together. And one thing that had replayed in her head, over and over, was how simple seeing him again could be if she kept it about sex. He felt obligated to explain the past to ensure the wedding went well. She'd take away the obligation.

She'd keep the simple, in the simple. The pleasure in the solution.

Mark sauntered up behind Marcie. "It's almost time for the games to begin. How about truth-or-dare to start?"

This might be an unconventional pre-wedding party, but it wasn't without conventional, naughty fun.

Marcie's eyes lit. "I can't wait." She turned in Mark's arms and fed him a bite of the strawberry. "In fact. I have all kinds of 'dares' I'd like you to personally perform."

Suddenly, Jennifer's skin prickled with awareness, the barely audible sound of Bobby's voice lifted from the depths of party fever, tingling a path up her spine. Instinctively, her gaze lifted the moment he filled the opening of the patio door, tall and broad, his presence demanding attention.

She allowed herself to devour him with her eyes, making no qualms about being obvious—after all, this was about sex, and she intended to make that clear in every possible way. Faded denim traced long, powerful thighs and accented a narrow waist. A button-down, navy-blue Western shirt outlined an equally impressive chest and, no doubt, covered a still impressive set of abs. He'd always had rock-hard, drool-worthy abs. And there was no denying, with Bobby's maturity, he'd become primitively sexual on some level she'd never consciously noticed before now.

But then, he wasn't the only one who'd matured. She was a woman, not a girl. She knew what she wanted and it was him. So did several other females gathering nearby, twentysomethings Jennifer didn't know, already tipsy and on the make for a man. They stared at him and giggled. But his eyes found Jennifer's, boldly telling, boldly sensual.

The music changed again to Marvin Gaye singing "let's make love tonight." She and Bobby stared at each other another second until they both smiled, and she knew they were both thinking the same thing—that they were going to make love tonight. The idea of sharing the same unspoken understanding in the middle of a crowd wasn't new for them—it was simply history. Working the moment, playing the seduction game, Jennifer turned away, knowing Bobby would join her. Anticipating it as eagerly as she was the prospect of stripping him naked and having her way with him. Well. Maybe not quite *that* much. But the process of getting from dressed to undressed was going to be oh so fun. It always was. She was going to let herself enjoy it. Oh, yes. Seducing Bobby was fun.

Marcie's wicked, mischief-filled expression settled on Jennifer. "We'll start getting the games together," she suggested, lacing her fingers with Mark's. "You enjoy yours."

Oh, she planned to, Jennifer thought.

Marcie and Mark disappeared about the time Bobby sauntered to Jennifer's side.

Jennifer inhaled his scent, awareness shimmering down her spine, as if her body had been conditioned to recognize his presence, and even that scent, as erotic. Oh, man. It had been a long time since she'd felt warm, wet heat spread between her thighs at the simple knowledge that a man she wanted was nearby.

Steeling herself for what would surely be another blast of white-hot arousal, she turned to face him. "You made it," she said in a remarkably unaffected voice, and motioned with her glass. "Drink?" She waved a hand at the table. "Or something to eat?"

"Just you," he said, stepping within inches of where she stood, inside the personal space reserved for lovers. As if he assumed he had that right before adding, in a low, husky voice bordering on possessive, "I came for you, Jennifer."

Jennifer's reaction was sudden, intense—all the white heat, pooling low and wicked in her stomach. "You came for Mark and Marcie," she corrected. "Like the rest of the guests."

"I'm going to the wedding for Mark and Marcie," he said, pinning her in a wicked stare. "I'm at this party to see you. The same reason I arrived for the wedding two weeks early."

No. She didn't want to hear that. Nor did she want to feel the twist in her gut, or the adrenaline surging inside her and setting her heart to thundering in her ears. Jennifer told herself to be as cool and unemotional as when she dealt with worried pet owners. She wouldn't react. It served no point.

But she did react. Before she could stop herself, she laughed, the sound crackling with a hint of bitterness she didn't want to admit existed. Jennifer tipped back her champagne and finished it off, trying to bite back words, the bubbles tickling her nose. Being the lightweight she was, she could tell it was going to go right to her head. She set the empty flute on the table, emotion welling in her chest, resentment with it.

Her hand flattened on the warm, hard wall of his chest, and she rose to her toes and brought her mouth an inch from his. She could almost taste him, and despite her anger, wanted just that. To taste him, to forget, to get lost.

"When you try to explain why you're here or why you left," she said, her voice a thick whisper, "I get mad, Bobby. So, if you want me, stop talking."

He covered her hand with his, his eyes dark, heavy-lidded. "I want you," he said, "but I won't stop talking until you hear what I have to say. And if that means you have to get mad, well, get mad. I can handle it."

"I can't," she said. "So I'll see you at the rehearsal dinner, and not until." She tried to shove him away.

He tugged her back, pulled her hard against his body, his hand molding her close. "We aren't done here yet."

"Says you," she said, entirely too breathless to appear unaffected.

"That's right," he half growled. "Says me."

"You don't get a say," she said. "Not since seven years ago when you left without a look back." Oh, hell, where had that come from?

His eyes narrowed instantly, his voice brusque. "I looked back every day of the past seven years."

"I don't want to hear this."

His jaw firmed and he started walking toward the house, pulling her with him. Jennifer didn't argue. He wanted to talk. Fine. They'd talk. Oh, yeah. Fine. Talk, talk, talk. She had plenty to say. Bring it on. Forget seduction. She wanted to yell, and yes, she wanted to throw something at him.

They were almost at the patio door when Sally, a petite brunette and waitress from the bar, appeared in the archway. "The police are here! They want Mark and Marcie!"

Jennifer's heart stopped. This couldn't be happening! They'd talked to the neighbors, and preapproved noise. Bobby turned to Jennifer.

She cast Bobby a pleading look. "Let me go. I have to stop the music!"

As if in response, the music stopped, and a blonde, curvy, female cop in uniform, with her hair pinned up, stepped through the sliding glass door, followed by a broad-shouldered, muscular male cop with lots of dark brown hair. The kind a girl runs her fingers through you didn't often see on a cop. Murmurs and muffled laughter followed, as if everyone was in on the joke but Jennifer.

"Ah, Jen," Bobby said, tugging her close to his side. "Is this what I think it is?"

"I hope not," she whispered. "I really, really hope not because Marcie and Mark were adamant they didn't want—"

Marcie skidded to a halt beside Jennifer, Mark on her heels. "What the heck is going on?"

"I'm looking for the owner of the house," the female cop said.

Bobby squeezed her hand in understanding of what was to come, as Mark stepped forward. "That would be me," Mark announced.

The female cop stared at Mark with a hard look and then walked toward him in a completely unsexual way that gave Jennifer hope this wasn't what she thought it was.

"I'm afraid we're going to have to ask you to turn down the volume on this party," the woman said. And oh boy, she got right up close to him. That wasn't comforting.

"Did someone complain?" Marcie asked quickly. "Because we talked to the neighbors, and—"

"I'm complaining," the male cop said, already closing in on Marcie. He stopped almost toe-to-toe with Marcie, towering over her as he added, "You can either turn down the volume or turn up the heat. I'm going to need you to report to the dance floor, ma'am."

Marcie's face paled as she blinked up at the cop. "What?" Then without looking at Jennifer, she said, "Jennifer?" A hint of panic laced her voice.

Jennifer got the panic part because she'd promised Marcie no strippers, and she was pretty sure the "cops" *were* strippers. And as maid of honor, it was Jennifer's job to fix this.

"There's been a mistake," Jennifer interjected and took a step forward, only to have Bobby pull her back, against him, his arm around her shoulders.

"It's too late," he said as she opened her mouth to object.

The way he'd anticipated her argument, the familiar way he touched her, the way he shared this experience with her as if he'd never left, shook her to the core.

And then to Jennifer's horror, the female cop reached up and let her hair free. Bobby chuckled. Jennifer cast him a warning look over her shoulder. She was in charge of this party and responsible for anything that went wrong.

In a blink, the entire situation spiraled to the point of no return. Marcie and Mark were herded to the dance floor and seated in chairs. All the guests huddled around them. Bobby and Jennifer stood behind it all, alone, side by side, but still close enough for a good visual.

"You should run," Jennifer said, "because Marcie is

going to want to blame me, and if you're nearby, you'll be guilty by association." Then, to Jennifer's shock, Marcie smacked the now mostly naked, male cop on the ass. Jennifer jumped. "Oh, my."

Bobby laughed. "I don't think she's mad, and judging from the way Mark is drooling, I don't think he's mad either."

Jennifer tilted her head and studied Mark. He looked heavy-lidded, definitely not mad. "This is just a little too weird for me," she said, turning away. "I can't watch. They're about to be married, and they're sharing lap dances. There is something so fundamentally wrong with that."

"We could go inside and play cops and robbers ourselves," he offered, wiggling a brow.

"I thought you were all about talking," she accused. "Not playing."

He pulled her close. "I told you," he corrected. "I'm all about you. Any way I can get you."

Narrowing her gaze, she studied him, her hands resting on his chest. "Talk is cheap," she said meaningfully. "Action counts. Sex without any strings. Take it or leave it."

His hand slid over her hip, and Jennifer felt the caress on every inch of her body. "What happened to not being my two-week fling?" he challenged.

Jennifer knew the answer all too well. In fact, she'd replayed this scene a hundred times over. "I decided to make you *my* two-week fling." And with that confession, she would have led him into the house, but suddenly a gasp went through the crowd.

"Where's the maid of honor?!" came a male voice. The cop, Jennifer realized. Or dancer. He wasn't a cop. Again he called out, "The bride wants the maid of honor. Where's Jennifer?"

"Oh, no," Jennifer said, turning to the crowd as they turned to her. Bobby released her, but stayed close. Instinct set Jennifer on edge just before her nerves proved merited. The male dancer appeared at the edge of the dance floor, facing Jennifer and Bobby, wearing nothing but an itty-bitty G-string.

"Are you the maid of honor?" he demanded, fixing Jennifer in a stare.

"Yes," the crowd replied. "That's her!"

"You'll need to report to the dance floor," he demanded. "Bride's orders."

"No way," Jennifer said. "No way!"

"I'm here to please the bride," the dancer assured her. "If you don't come willingly, I'll have to take you by force."

"Oh, hell no," Bobby grumbled at the same moment her fight-or-flight instinct sent Jennifer into flight. Which went horribly. Jennifer tripped over her own feet and reached out to catch herself. Her hands plodded, with a splash, into two large bowls of chocolate mousse. She screamed on impact.

Bobby's arm wrapped around her waist, pulling her toward him seconds before her face would have landed in the ranch dip. Her hands came out of the chocolate sauce, dripping, messy. She gasped as Bobby picked her up and started carrying her toward the house, cradling her like a baby. A good thing since she didn't dare hold on, awkwardly dangling her hands in the air. She glanced at them and then up at Bobby, at the strong, determined set of his jaw. He laughed, a deep, playful sound that resonated through her, turning her all warm and wanting when she should be indignant. And she was.

"Don't you dare laugh!" she declared, as he maneuvered them past the sliding glass door and headed to the kitchen.

"I can't help myself," he said, walking into the forest-green-and-black-tiled kitchen.

"You *can* help yourself."

"Sweetheart," he said, "if you dip yourself in chocolate when I'm around, you have two options. I laugh. Or I lick it off." He set her down in front of the sink, facing him. His voice lowered, his gaze intense, as he raised one of her fingers to his mouth and nibbled. "Or both."

Her breath lodged in her throat, and she coughed once, twice. Getting her man and her chocolate sauce hadn't gone exactly as planned. But she wasn't about to complain, not when he was leaning forward about to kiss her.

6

JENNIFER'S ANNOUNCEMENT that she planned to make him her two-week fling, to dismiss him with sex, pissed Bobby off in all kinds of ways. But it also worked in his favor. Because he knew what she would soon find out. Sex was the erotic, emotional path they would travel to get to a locked door on their past.

Bobby stared down at Jennifer. The only thing keeping him from setting her up on the counter, stepping between her legs, and then kissing her until there was no tomorrow, was the chocolate all over her hands.

Oh, hell. Who cared about a mess? They'd shower later—together. He reached for Jennifer, right when a giant clump of chocolate dropped onto his boot. Jennifer glanced down. Bobby did, as well. Their gazes lifted and collided as they both smiled.

"Hmm, sorry," she said. "I should probably clean up before I make matters worse."

His lips twitched. "As appealing as I find licking chocolate off you," he agreed, "I do prefer a more strategic placement."

Jennifer smiled. He loved her smile. All Texas sunrise

and honey. She blew hair from her eyes and rotated to face the sink. He turned it on for her and she agreed, "Definitely nothing strategic about falling in the party food while being chased by a cop, who's really a lap dancer, and who isn't even supposed to be here."

"Marcie and Mark don't seem to care," Bobby said, cleaning off his boot, his gaze sliding over Jennifer's lush, heart-shaped backside. Tension waved through his body, sexual, hot. Ravishing. Like he wanted to ravish her.

"Marcie isn't happy," Jen assured him. "Otherwise, she wouldn't have sent that dancer to drag me to hell with her." She turned off the water and grabbed a towel.

"Marcie knew I'd never let that dancer anywhere near you," he said, as he stepped behind her, framing her petite curves with his body, and pressing his hands on the sink beside her. She drew a surprised breath and then grabbed the counter. "Just as I never should have allowed anyone else near you in the first place. I missed you, Jen." He buried his face in the silky strands of her long blond hair, erotic memories of having it sprayed across his chest shaking him to the core. There was more than want in him for Jennifer. There was need.

"Don't," she whispered. "Don't say things like that."

"I can't help myself," he confessed, meaning it. One of his hands slid to her stomach, and Bobby's gut clenched with the memories of intimacy, of holding her, of burying himself inside her and hearing her call his name. He wanted to hear her call his name again. Over and over.

Her hand pressed down on his. "We agreed no

talking," she reminded him, but her voice lacked conviction.

"Just sex," he said flatly, but there was a crackle beneath the surface.

"Yes," she confirmed softly, "just sex."

He used both hands, a double assault, caressing a path over her slender waist, brushing the curve of her breasts, and then molding them to his palms. "Is this what you want?" he asked.

She made a strangled sound and her head fell back to his shoulder. "Yes," she whispered.

He inhaled her scent, teasing her nipples through the sheer fabric. "I remember your scent—jasmine," he said. "Delicious and sweet." He shoved aside the thin material and tweaked one of her nipples. She shivered in his arms. The nipple knotted to his touch. He remembered well. "You know what else I remember?"

"I don't want to know," she said. "No memories."

"I remember how wet you get when I touch your breasts and lick them. If I tease them just right, you'll come right here in the kitchen."

"I will not," she gasped.

He shoved both sides of her shirt down, bra along with it. Tugged on both stiff peaks. She moaned. "Want to bet on that?" he asked.

"Yes," she hissed on a soft sound of pleasure that defied her words. "I bet on that."

A low, desire-laden laugh rumbled in his throat. "Did you forget how much I enjoy a good challenge?" He picked her up, turned her and set her on the counter, spreading her legs in the process. He feasted on the sight of her high, full breasts and then pressed them together to lave on a nipple. "You still think I can't make you come?"

Jennifer was panting, her hands pressed to the counter behind her, holding her up. She bit her bottom lip. "It's, no…if I come, it's because—"

He lapped at her nipple. "Because it's me?" He framed her face with his hands. "Because it's us?"

She blinked up at him. "Stop using sex as a weapon," she whispered.

"Isn't that what *you* planned to do?" he demanded. "Use sex to keep me at a distance?" And he couldn't let her do that, not with only two weeks until the biggest decision of his life, since leaving Jennifer seven years ago. Reenlist or stay? "You should have known that wouldn't work. We were too good together. We still are."

"You of all people should know," she hissed, "that sometimes sex is a way to an orgasm. It's just sex."

There it was—the gauntlet thrown down, the accusation that she'd meant nothing to him, which cut like a finely sharpened blade. "Is that all you think we were?" he demanded. "Sex?"

Her chin lifted. "Wasn't it?"

Frustration mixed with urgency inside Bobby as the music shifted to a country song, voices suddenly carrying inside the house. An indicator the show was over and their alone time was ending.

"No matter how we ended, Jennifer," he told her, his tone guttural, "we were real." Bobby kissed her, long and hard. "And I'm not going to let you forget that." He pulled Jennifer's shirt back into place. And not a moment too soon.

Marcie's voice bellowed from the near distance. "Jennifer!"

"This isn't over," Bobby told her, setting her on the ground. "Not even close."

"Don't bet on that one, Bobby," Jennifer said. "You'll lose."

"It's time to play truth-or-dare," Marcie said from the doorway, with an intoxicated giggle.

Bobby leaned close to Jennifer. "I dare you to finish what we started," Bobby said, and he wasn't talking sex, though sex was fine by him. He was talking everything—the past, the present, the future. Bobby turned to Marcie. "Let the games begin."

MARCIE SHOUTED ACROSS the backyard to have the music stopped, ready to start the games. She giggled and turned back to Jennifer. "Let's get ready to rumble!"

Jennifer held her hand over her face. There was no rumbling in the game of truth-or-dare, but there was plenty of rumble to Jennifer's nerves. Like it wasn't enough that she'd already delved into the "sex as a weapon" game with Bobby and lost round one. Now she had a tipsy Marcie to contend with.

Marcie grabbed Jennifer's hand and tugged her onward. "Let's go," she said. "This is going to be so fun."

Fifteen minutes later, Jennifer hadn't seen hide nor hair of Bobby. The game was about to begin, and this other game, the one between Bobby and herself, was clearly well under way. A huge circle of twenty guests sat on a carpet runner circling the dance floor, ready to play truth-or-dare.

Marcie sat next to Mark, and patted the rug on her opposite side. "Come, Jen!"

Jennifer sat down, scanning for Bobby, and silently scolding herself for the disappointment curling in her stomach at his disappearance. Had he left? And why? Why did she care? *Because she wanted that orgasm he'd almost given her,* she declared in her mind, refusing to allow any other answer to be considered.

As if Bobby sensed her feelings, he appeared directly across from her, behind Scott Wright, a neighbor down the road, who was already seated. Jennifer's heart charged into action as Bobby bent down and whispered to Scott. A second later, Scott got up and Bobby claimed his seat.

Bobby arched a brow at Jennifer, letting her know he was ready for round two of "sex as a weapon." Jennifer couldn't move, the sound around her fading, the tension, wholly sexual, snapping between her and Bobby like a rubber band. Everything inside Jennifer melted like chocolate in the hot sun. She was the chocolate and he was the hot sun, when the opposite had been her plan.

Marcie elbowed Jennifer, none too subtly. "It's Bobby," she whispered. "Did you see Bobby?"

Jennifer cringed. Bobby looked amused, his eyes twinkling with mischief, the corners of his lips hinting at a smile. His really sexy lips, the ones that had been on hers only a short while back. Her nipples tightened, ached, her breasts growing heavy. Okay, those lips had been on a whole lot more than her mouth.

Marcie rang a bell. Where had she gotten a bell? And a loud one, ringing near Jennifer's ear. Jennifer reached for it and silently vowed to pour the rest of that chocolate mousse over the head of whoever gave it to her. "Give me that," Jennifer ordered.

"I need it," Marcie said. Mark tugged Marcie close to him and took the bell.

"Thank you, Mark," Jennifer said, feeling relieved until Mark started whistling louder than the bell. Oh, good grief.

The crowd quieted and Marcie waved like a schoolgirl. "Hi, everyone," Marcie said, laughing as they all stared at her. She draped herself over Jennifer's shoulders and ran her hand down Jennifer's hair. "Tell them how the game words, Jen." Marcie hiccupped. "I mean works."

Bobby's stare, brimming with understanding, met Jennifer's.

Jennifer sighed and gently eased Marcie off her. "This is how the game works," Jennifer told the crowd. "We have a board, dice and two stacks of cards that we pass around the circle. Odd number draws. One dare card. One truth card. You choose one or the other."

Marcie held up a finger and called out, "Adding a new rule!" She eyed Jennifer. "It's the bride's prerogative." Then she peered around the circle. "If you don't want either card, you have to strip off one item of clothing."

Jennifer gaped, shook her head. This was where she drew the line. She started to get up. Marcie grabbed her arm. "Oh, no, you don't." Then to the circle of guests, "The maid of honor is trying to run out on us, you guys."

Shouts rang out. Demands that Jennifer "be a man" and stay for the game. Like she wanted to "be a man." Nevertheless, she was hogtied into staying.

Marcie gloated, then announced. "The wedding party will go first! Come on, Jen, loosen up."

Jennifer had gotten plenty loose in that kitchen with Bobby, and she had no intention of getting loose in the middle of a crowd. She didn't even consider looking in Bobby's direction on that one. Instead, she lashed back at Marcie.

"Bride and groom go first!" Jennifer yelled.

Marcie's eyes lit. "Okay!"

So much for lashing back. Marcie rolled the dice. Even number. No card draw for her. She slid the board to Mark, who quickly rolled the dice. Odd number. He drew two cards.

Marcie giggled in anticipation. "Read the cards to everyone," she said anxiously.

"Truth card," Mark said. "Who is the best lover you have ever had?" He grinned and looked at Marcie.

She smiled. "Read the other one."

"Dare card," Mark said. "Perform a striptease for the room." His eyes widened. "I'll take the truth. Marcie is the best lover I have ever had."

Everyone booed, yelling that he'd gotten off easy. "I'm the groom," Mark declared. "That's how it should work. At least until I walk down the aisle."

Marcie gaped and he grinned. "Just joking." He bent down and gave Marcie a quick kiss.

The next person was Sally, who was not only in the wedding, but the one Jennifer was pretty darn sure had ordered the dancers. Sally rolled an odd number. She drew two cards. "Truth. Have you ever used a vibrator?" She crinkled her nose. "Dare. Kiss the person to your right. Must use tongue." That person was Mark. Holy crap. This was not going well.

Marcie grabbed Jennifer's arm, digging her finger-nails through her bare flesh. "Aye," Jennifer complained but Marcie didn't let go.

Everyone stared at Sally, the time ticking by in slow, excruciating seconds. Sally bit her lip and then said, "Truth. Sometimes a good vibrator is better than a man who doesn't know what he is doing."

A general sigh of relief fell across the lawn. As if everyone knew how bad the bad would have been if Sally would have kissed Mark.

It was the best man's turn and he ended up with a dare. He mooned the circle. Another bridesmaid stripped off her shirt, leaving her in her bra. A grooms-man and bridesmaid who Jennifer thought hated each other kissed, with tongue action, and now it was Bobby's turn.

He rolled the dice. Odd number. His eyes met Jennifer's from across the circle. Anticipation thrummed through her veins.

"Truth," he said. "What is the kinkiest thing you ever did with a feather?"

A slow smile spread on his lips, but he didn't look up. She knew exactly what he was thinking and felt her cheeks redden. Once, years before, he'd tied her face-down on the bed and, well, the feather had driven her insane. Surely he wouldn't tell that story? Then again, he'd had seven years to use feathers in all kinds of ways she might never even dream possible. Her heart sank.

"Dare," he said, glancing down at the card. "Drink four shots of tequila."

He stared at the card and Jennifer's stomach twisted. He wouldn't drink four shots of anything stronger than Kool-Aid. The man could nurse one beer all night long and make everyone think it was his third or fourth. At least, the Bobby she'd known seven years ago.

He'd said it was about control, but she'd always suspected it was about his father being a drinker. But he'd never talked about it, and shut down when she'd tried. *He hadn't talked about it,* she repeated in her mind. He'd never really let her inside. It—they really had been all about sex.

Several women started chanting at Bobby, "Shirt, shirt, shirt. Take off your shirt."

Slowly, Bobby's gaze lifted to Jennifer's, and he reached down and took off his boot. Boos followed. He took off a second boot. "That's all you get," he said sternly.

Relief washed over Jennifer. She didn't have to find out if his feather story would be about her or someone else. She didn't have to endure sharing a view of that hot, broad chest with the crowd. Her relief, however, was short-lived as the shouts began, "Jennifer is next. Jennifer is next!"

She ground her teeth. The history between Bobby and herself was far from a secret to many of the long-term friends at the party.

Before Jennifer could blink, the board and dice were in front of her. Fine. She wanted this over with. She rolled the dice. Seven. Which used to be her lucky number. But it was an odd number. Of course. Not lucky tonight. She had to draw cards. "Truth," she said, reading the first one. "When was the last time you…" She all but choked. There was no way she was reading the rest of the card or answering the question.

Marcie grabbed the card and finished for her. "Had an orgasm, and who or what gave it to you?"

If Jennifer admitted she'd given her last orgasm to herself, last night, Bobby was sure to assume it was while fantasizing about him. Which it was, or had been. And most certainly could be again.

"Dare," she said, snatching another card and reading it out loud. "Straddle the person to your right, male or female, while giving them tongue action."

"Or strip!" Marcie said. "And no boots like Bobby." Marcie glared at Bobby. "That was a copout!"

Jennifer's heart lurched as she stared at that card, feeling the magnetic pull of Bobby's stare, as he willed her to look at him. And realizing she didn't even know who was sitting next to her—that was how fixated she'd been on Bobby. She looked to her right. To the guy sitting next to her who had chin-length brown hair, full lips and deep brown eyes. Good-looking.

He extended his hand, as if she needed a formal introduction before cramming her tongue down his throat. "David," he said. "Mark's college roommate. Feel free to take advantage of me any way you please."

Jennifer stared at his hand, realizing she had an opportunity. A way to draw the line in the sand with Bobby. To make it clear she didn't want, or need, fluffy explanations and conversation. Kissing David would let Bobby know she was over everything between them but the sex. Okay, so maybe, just maybe, a part of her wanted to lash out and hurt Bobby. The way he'd hurt her. Of course, damn him, she doubted she could hurt him. And that hurt her. Jennifer was going to kiss David. She slid her hand into his.

7

JENNIFER'S PLAN TO kiss David lasted all of thirty seconds before she was suddenly pulled into Bobby's strong arms. Anger radiated off him, his voice low, serious, "If you're trying to piss me off," he declared, lacing his fingers in her hair, his blue eyes glinting with steel, "it's working." His mouth slanted over hers, punishing, hard, full of demand.

Jennifer told herself not to respond, to shove him away, but the thrust of his tongue against hers, the spicy, primitive taste of him, ignited something inside her. So, instead of resisting, she kissed him back, answering the anger spilling through him, into her, with anger of her own. Kissed him with the kind of passion that could not be bred of mere physical attraction, the kind of attraction formed from an emotional bond, once built, and then torn down. Kissed him with every drop of emotion curled inside her, ready to explode—with seven years of anger and hurt, with the devastation of the night he'd left, and the determination to send him away again, but on her terms.

Time stood still as she poured all the shattered pieces

of herself into the slide of tongue against tongue. Her hands gripped his shoulders, one to his face. She took… and took; she demanded.

It was Bobby who broke the connection, pulling back to stare down at her with dark eyes that stole a path straight to her soul. Jennifer could barely breathe, compelled by their intensity, in the certainty that whatever escape she'd believed the kiss had offered, had simply led her deeper into a trap.

Bobby pushed to his feet and for the second time that evening, he scooped her into his arms. The crowd came back into focus, the hoots and hollers suddenly an invasion of privacy. Jennifer buried her face in Bobby's neck, seeking refuge with the very man she should be hiding from. But what she felt, what she wanted, what she had to deal with—all of it ended right back at him and him alone, not to be shared with anyone else. Not a crowd, not even Marcie, who was like a sister to her.

Jennifer let him carry her away, knowing full well they were headed to a bedroom to finish what they'd started seven years before. In bed. And she was going to enjoy every last minute of it—because she deserved it.

BOBBY WAS ANGRY. No. Angry didn't begin to touch on the wild emotions spiraling inside him, the possessiveness. Everything male in him wanted to claim her, had to claim her, though he knew he had no right—that he'd left, that he'd given her up. But reason didn't matter right now. Feeling her close, holding her, being with her, making love to her—that was what mattered.

At first, a little gamesmanship offered a good chance to use a few skydiving dares and he'd get to combine work with pleasure. It meant assurance that he could get out to the Hotzone, and investigate this ex-Army Ranger Rocky, without losing his leave time with Jennifer. He wanted his mission complete, done, over and quickly. But despite his urgency to get focused on Jennifer, Bobby was all about checking out this Rocky character. One thing Bobby couldn't stand was a man who fought for his country, turning against his country. And if Rocky was selling drugs, he was definitely working against his country.

Bobby carried Jennifer up the stairs, taking them two at a time. He shoved open a spare bedroom, dim light flickering from a bedside lamp. He kicked the door shut behind them, locked it, and carried Jennifer to the mattress. They went down on the bed, her on the bottom, him on top. That was where he wanted to be. On top. For now. Later, she could be on top.

"What was that all about down there?" he demanded. "On second thought, don't answer that. You'll just piss me off more than I already am."

"You're pissed—" He smothered her words with a kiss, spearing his tongue past her lips with command. She was his, maybe not forever, but for now. He branded her with long strokes of his tongue, greedily taking until he tore his mouth from hers, hungry for more than her mouth.

She gasped and shoved at his shoulders. "You're pissed off?" she demanded. "I'm pissed off, Bobby!"

"Good," he hissed and pushed off the bed, unbuttoning his shirt enough to pull it over his head. "Then show me pissed off, Jennifer. Show me now." He tossed the shirt on the floor. He remembered the fights and the makeup sex—passionate, hot, couldn't-get-enough-of-each-other sex—he wanted that now.

Jennifer pressed herself to a sitting position on the bed, her breath heavy, chest rising and falling, lifting her full, high breasts, as she declared, "This isn't makeup sex, Bobby," she warned, reading his mind. Proving she still knew him.

Shackling her ankles, he pulled her to the end of the bed, her legs on either side of his, her back now on the mattress. Hands to her waist, Bobby pushed her shirt upward and made quick work of removing it. "Fine then," he said, grabbing one of her boots, and then the other, insurance she wasn't going anywhere fast. "It's not makeup sex."

She sat up and pressed her hands to his waist, tilting her chin to stare up at him with a gleam in her beautiful eyes. "Then it's settled," she said, her hand sliding over his crotch, tracing the rock-hard ridge of his bulging erection before unsnapping his pants. "Just sex. Only sex. And I'm in charge." She tugged his zipper down, then tugged at his waist. "Take them off."

He didn't argue. The faster they were naked, the happier he would be. He wanted to be inside her. He wanted to taste her. He wanted to fuck her and then make love to her and do them both again, in no particular order. Fully intending to undress, he instead stood spellbound, watching Jennifer as she undressed. His cock thickened as her bra fell away, her nipples plump and rosy, with memories of licking them while she sat on the kitchen counter.

Next she stood, sliding down her jeans and panties, kicking them aside. And how had he gone seven years without seeing this woman naked? Desire punched him in the stomach with gut-wrenching impact, his gaze raking over soft ivory skin, a narrow waist, sexy hips.

He reached for her. She held up a hand and side-stepped. "Oh, no, Bobby. You want control but you don't have it." She was behind him before he knew her intention, her hands on his waist. "Slide these jeans down and let me see if your backside is still as glorious as it once was."

His cock twitched, as pleased with her comment as he was. "You thought my backside was glorious?" he asked over his shoulder, shoving his pants down, underwear and all.

"You know I did," she said, and he could hear the smile in her voice.

He grinned. "Yeah," he admitted, since she'd told him often. "But I wanted to hear you say it." Because it reminded her of the past, because it drove home how much that past was a part of the sex they were about to have. And because it did his ego good.

Jennifer smacked his ass, not hard, but it got him harder—as if that was even possible, but apparently it was. Electric heat raced down his thighs, tugged at his balls.

"Nice and firm," she purred. "I approve."

He would have reached for her, but she seemed to anticipate his intentions and wrapped herself around him. He damn near whimpered. This was Jennifer—soft, silky Jennifer who had melted into him like a second skin, the stiff peaks of her nipples against his back, her hands on his stomach.

He reached down, grabbed her hand and pulled her forward. Molded her to his side and chest, her hip resting against his jutting erection.

She reached down and stroked it. He sucked in a breath and molded her closer. "I liked this, too," she said, closing her hand around the width. He pulsed in her hand, and offered her a little of her own medicine, smacking her ass, as she had his.

She gasped and pumped his cock. He laced his fingers in her hair and kissed her, drank in that sweet, honey bliss and suckled her tongue. She was on her toes, reaching for more of his mouth, her hand working him over. Oh, yes, she was still a mind-blowing combination of sweet angel who could turn sex goddess behind closed doors.

He closed his hand over hers. "If this is your way of punishing me for the ass slap, sweetheart," he said, "please, don't stop."

"I can think of so many better ways to punish you," she promised.

"Any of them involve a feather?" he challenged. "And yes—I remember that feather often, and there is no way I would have shared our secrets. What we do together is between us."

She blinked up at him, the tension suddenly thick between them—sexual, emotional, raw. And then something snapped. The games, all of them, outside the room, and inside, were gone.

"Jennifer," he said softly, lifting her weight so that her legs wrapped around his waist.

Her hand went to his face, her fingers lacing his jaw, his lips. "I can't believe you're really here," she whispered.

Bobby sucked in a breath, his chest heavy with the impact of her words, at the message behind them. She'd told him more than she realized. This moment, them together again, meant something more to her than sex. And he burned to spill the regret in his heart, to explain why he'd left. To open a door for them to explore what might be in their future. Instinctively though, he knew, if he said the wrong thing, she'd shut down. He'd lose the ground he'd gained.

As much as Bobby knew she wanted control, he needed to feel her beneath him. He settled her on the mattress, and went down on top of her, urging her legs apart as he pressed between them. For tonight, she was his.

Clarity wrenched through him before he pressed his erection to the V of her body where wet heat enveloped him in pure bliss. He sucked in a breath. "Please tell me you're still on the pill," he said, willing himself to move, but unable to find the will. "Because I left the condoms I bought in the car."

"You bought condoms?" she asked. "Assuming we would—"

He kissed her. "Hoping."

"I'm on the pill," she whispered.

Her admission hit him with a hard dose of bittersweet emotion. Bobby swallowed a lump the size of Texas. Part of him screamed with the reality of her being on the pill to be with other men. Of course, he knew this, expected it. He'd left. He'd handed her over. He'd been with other women. But none who touched him as Jen had, still did. And he was damn lucky no other man had married her and made babies. That no other man had crossed the lines of intimacy he'd shared with her.

And so he kissed her, a long sweep of his tongue drawing hers into action. Wildness unleashed in him, a fierce need to make her his—a fierce demand that she *was* his, no matter how false that statement, no matter how untrue it might be.

His hand traveled her rib cage, her breasts. He pinched her nipples, tugged and tweaked, feeling her arch against him, her thighs clenching as she tried to pull his cock deep into the wet heat of her body. Silently begging him to enter her. And how he wanted inside her, but he also wanted this to last. Bobby tore his mouth from hers, maneuvering so that he lay beside her, and then angling her forward, intending to put her on her stomach.

"Oh, no," she said. "You. On your back. I told you. I'm in charge."

"Me, doing anything and everything to please you," he said, his hand sliding down her hip, lips nuzzling her neck, teeth nipping her earlobe. "If that's not control, I don't know what is." He brushed her hair aside, kissing her neck, urging her to her stomach. He smiled against her skin. "You can still tell me exactly where you want me." His lips brushed her skin again. "Exactly what you need."

And what he needed—was her.

8

JENNIFER DIDN'T BUY the "pleasure was control" bit Bobby gave her, no matter how tempting lying down and just letting Bobby please her might be. And Bobby *could* please her. She had no doubt. But she wanted him on her terms. That was what this night was about; that was how it had started and that was how it would end. Besides, exploring every delectable inch of his hotness wasn't something she planned to miss. And he was hot, hotter than when he'd left—all man, all grown up, in all the right places. And she couldn't do that exploring on her stomach.

Rotating around to face Bobby, both of them on their sides, Jennifer slid her hip under the jutted thickness of his erection as she urged him to his back. "I'm on top," she insisted, reaching down to stroke his cock, sliding her fingers onto the sleek proof of just how ready he was for her. Her lips settled a breath from his. "Take it or leave it."

He tugged her close, molding her to hard muscle. Their breath mingled, warm and tempting. "I'll take you any way I can get you," he said, his lips brushing hers, the soft caress sliding along every nerve ending she owned.

Barely containing a shiver, she whispered, "Good." Then more forcefully, she ordered, "Now. On your back. Hands behind your head. You touch when I say you touch."

He did as she said, cock standing up, engorged, inviting her to climb on top, to finally feel him inside her again. Instead, she scooted close to his side, flattening her hand on his abdomen, the ripples of hard muscle flexing beneath her fingers. Desire welled inside her.

Stretched out, he was six foot three inches of long, hard male, waiting for her next move. "What should I do first?" she queried mischievously, sitting up and running a hand over one powerful thigh.

"I'll be happy to offer suggestions," he said, his voice deep, raspy, his eyes raking over her nipples. They puckered instantly, the reaction spreading through her body and pooling heat between her thighs.

"I bet you can," she said, her palm traveling up his hip, over his pelvis, teasing him with how close she was to the jut of his erection. "Like taking you in my mouth, I bet." She knew how much talking turned him on. It did her, too.

"Suck me, baby," he said. "Put those sweet lips around me and end my misery."

She leaned in slowly. "Maybe I prefer you in misery," she said, kissing his stomach, her hair spraying tantalizingly across his cock, teasing him. And she knew it, and enjoyed every second. She wrapped her palm around the base of his shaft, glancing up at him as she blew lightly on the tip.

"Witch," he accused, his hips lifting toward her mouth.

With her tongue, she dotted the head of his shaft, and he moaned. "Wicked witch," she promised, wrapping the width of him with her hand, when suddenly, he moved.

Before she knew what was happening, Bobby had the V of her body at his head and his mouth closed down on her. She gasped as he suckled her clit, her hand tightening on his cock.

She rolled into him, so that they were facing one another, on their sides, and drew him into her mouth, suckling him as he laved her with his tongue, teasing the sensitive flesh. His fingers slid inside her, stretching her, pleasuring her.

Jennifer suckled Bobby deeper, harder, her mind a rainbow of colors, all about need, want, desire—for more of Bobby. She moaned as little darts of sensation slid down her thighs, up her stomach, into her breasts. One hand held him firmly, the other grabbed his backside, pulling him into her, taking him deeper. He pumped against her slide, up and down his length. Faster, harder. His fingers stroked her inside, his tongue licked her, lips suckled her clit.

"Oh," she moaned, the rush of heat coming over her in a sudden, intense blast. Unable to breathe with the pleasure building inside her, she let go of him with all but her hand. Jennifer collapsed against his stomach in a shuddered release that shot through her core and shook her body until she gasped with the final spasm that left her seeing stars.

"Damn you," she whispered, lifting her head, so limp and loose, she could barely move. "I was—"

He cut off her words with actions, smiling and rolling her to her back, spreading her legs, braced above her as he slid his cock along her wet aching core. "On top," he said, finishing her sentence. "Now I'm on top." He slipped the head of his shaft inside her and then thrust deep. "And inside you where we both want me to be." Slowly, holding her stare, Bobby slid his pulsing cock back down the sleek, wet canal of her body, until only the head remained. Jennifer arched her hips, reaching for him, whispering a plea. He was driving her crazy with anticipation. Bobby drove into her.

Sensation exploded in the depths of her womb and Jennifer gasped, her fingers curling on Bobby's biceps, as he buried himself to the hilt. Without warning, emotion shoved its way to the surface. Bobby inside her. The man she'd once thought was her world. The man she would have said only two days ago, she never wanted to see again.

And yet he was here, resting on his elbows, looming above her in all his naked glory. They stared at each other, his expression shadowy, taut, filled with torment that spoke of so much more than simple lust and passion.

Jennifer squeezed her eyes shut. No. This was sex. She could enjoy sex. She could walk away from sex. Sex did not leave her emotionally drained and hurt.

Determination formed inside her and Jennifer's lashes snapped open. She arched her hips against his, her arms wrapping around his neck, chest pressed to his.

"Now, Bobby," she ordered, knowing how close to the edge he had to be. How ready for release.

He didn't argue with her demand. He gave her what

she wanted, kissing her, claiming her mouth with a wild, hot kiss, and thrusting into her body. Emotion splintered into need, dissolving inside the shuddering ache blistering her inside and out. Bobby lifted one of her legs, angling her to drive harder into her, but still it wasn't enough.

"More," she whispered hoarsely, her lips pressing on his chest, his neck, his chin. "I want more."

He drew back and stared down at her, something dark sliding across his face, before his mouth was on hers, his palm over her breast. On her body. Ruthlessly touching her, drawing her toward the point of no return. She could taste the change in him, the absoluteness of his need vibrating through the tension of his body. It turned her on, exploded inside her, the way she burned for him, too.

She bucked against him. She had to have more, more. "Harder," she gasped.

He pressed her knees to her chest and gave her what she wanted. Hard pumps, fast pumps, deep pumps—his cock driving into her. Bobby driving into her. She needed Bobby. More. Now. She panted, trying to speak again but there were no words. Orgasm came over her in a sudden explosion. Jennifer fingers dug into Bobby's forearms, her muscles clutching at his cock, shaking her entire body.

Bobby let out a guttural growl, pounding into her one last time, his head tilting back as the taut muscles in his body shook with release, warm heat spilling inside her. Jennifer was spellbound, watching him, riveted by the sleek lines of taut, defined muscle flexing with his release. The intensity of his expression. And yes, the bittersweet bliss of Bobby on top of her, inside her, with her.

He collapsed on top of her, head buried in her neck. She clung to him, too, told herself not to, but the minute she let him go, the minute they spoke or moved, the mood would shift. The reality would pierce the fantasy.

The air thickened with unspoken words—he felt it, too, she sensed that in him. The need to say something, to explain, to make the past better, when there was no possible way he could. But lying there, the heavy weight of him resting so erotically on top of her, she wished he could. Wished there were a way.

Long seconds later, Bobby eased off her, his gaze brushing past hers, as if he were afraid to look at her. And when she might have escaped, he pulled her back to his chest, strong arms surrounding her, his powerful leg sliding intimately over one of hers. His lips nuzzling her neck. And she let him. Let him move her, let him hold her. Let herself enjoy the moment. Until the moment was gone, and reality arrived.

"The night I left," he said finally, "my old man was arrested."

The announcement shocked her. His father had been arrested, and she had never known. She could hear her heart thundering in her ears as she thought about that evening—shopping with Marcie, lighthearted, having fun. Then the hours later when Bobby wouldn't take her calls, when she feared something was wrong with him. And finally, when something deep in her heart had known he was gone for good, but logic had said she was insane—they were in love, they were getting married.

"He was drunk," Bobby continued. "And he drove

his truck into a house. A young mother and her son were inside, and barely escaped injury. I knew he'd had a problem for years. Hell, he was the reason I got good grades and a scholarship to college in Austin. I wanted out of San Antonio, out of that house. And I wasn't about to be held captive by money. When I got out, I was out. I didn't want to ever go back. And I made damn sure I kept you away from that world and, most importantly, my father."

He drew a breath and Jennifer found herself letting out the one she was holding. Bobby continued, "But that night, when he called me from jail, I drove to San Antonio and I tried to help him. To convince him to agree to rehab. His attorney was backing me. That was when my uncle showed up. Joe. I never introduced you to Joe. He's a drinker like my father. A real bastard when he's had too much—which is pretty much always. Joe teamed up with my father, said I thought I was better than them. Joe said he'd been to college, too, and it wouldn't save me. That I would end up like him sooner than later. It was a hot spot for me. My worst fear. What if I became like them?

"I got in the car and started driving again but not back to Austin. Hell, I didn't even know where I was going. I blinked and I was five hundred miles away, somewhere near the Mexican border, and there was an Army recruiting office. It felt like a sign, the thing I was supposed to do. I was ashamed. I didn't want you to know what had happened, or what I was destined to become. A random drunk in San Antonio would never make the Austin papers and I told no one. And so I made the choice to save lives so I wouldn't destroy them. Or you. So I couldn't destroy you. I loved you too much."

His breath caught, a long, tension-laden pause, before he added, "And I knew…I knew, Jen, if I saw you again, I'd be too weak to walk away."

Jennifer lay there, unmoving, incapable of words, her heart lodged in her throat. Trying to digest what she really knew about Bobby. His mother had passed away from cancer when he was in his teens, and Jennifer had met his father several times, usually at the bar up the road from his shop. She'd known his father was a drinker, and she'd known it bothered Bobby. But yet, she had known nothing about how bad it was for him at home, about how bad the night he'd left had been. He'd shut her out. Maybe he'd never let her in, in the first place.

Jennifer could feel herself unraveling inside, wrestling with the heaviness in her chest, the thickness in her throat. Until an explosion of emotion burst from her, adrenaline sending her into action. Jennifer pushed out of his arms—or tried. Bobby held her too closely, the intimacy of seconds before now ringing more like captivity.

"Jennifer—"

"Let me up, Bobby!"

"Jen—"

"Let. Me. Up!"

He did. He let her go and Jennifer bolted. She whirled around on her knees, oblivious to her nakedness. She opened her mouth to speak and found she couldn't. Not without crying. He'd never really given himself to her. He'd been looking for a reason to run and found it in his father.

"There hasn't been a day—" he started.

"…you haven't regretted leaving," she finished for

him, going cold inside. She'd spent seven years hurting over this man. Seven years hoping for a reason that would make sense besides that he needed an excuse out. "We just slept together, Bobby. The last time I checked, orgasm doesn't require conversation." She gave him a disdainful look. "But right now, I need to get back to Marcie. I'm in charge of the party."

She scrambled toward the edge of the bed and just barely escaped as he reached for her. "So that's it?" he challenged. "I'm letting it all hang out here, Jennifer, and you're blowing me off?"

"Isn't that what you did to me for seven years?" she asked, giving him her back. He didn't respond, but he would. The air was thick, the tension crackling. But he was dressing, too; he was preparing to head her off before she departed. A confrontation was coming, and it wasn't going to be all joy and bliss like being naked in that bed had been.

Struggling with her last boot, not about to risk the vulnerability of sitting on the bed where he might end up on top of her again—and Lord help her, she might just decide to rip her clothes off again, in the name of "she deserved every damn bit of pleasure he could give her"—Jennifer lost her balance. Bobby reached for her.

"Don't!" she bit out, righting herself. "Don't touch me, Bobby." She glared at him, looking at him directly for the first time since she started dressing.

Before she knew what happened, he was there, pulling her hard against his body, powerful arms wrapping around her, his long legs entwining with hers. "I'm going to touch you, Jen. And kiss you and make love to you. I'm not asking permission either. I have less than two weeks to prove to you how much you mean to me, and I fully intend to succeed."

Defiance rose inside her, the need to lash out, to find a way to protect herself. And running kept backfiring. "Of course you will," she said, casting him a look from beneath her lashes, playing coy, her anger banked. "That's why it's called a fling. You please me. I please you. And then it's over, and life goes on."

His jaw set, his expression taut. His hands framed her face. "You don't believe that any more than I do."

She could feel herself shaking inside with the challenge, but she tilted her chin up, challenged him. "Believe it," she said softly, her voice edged with a hint of steel she couldn't quite suppress. "Because, you see, unlike you, I know when to say goodbye. I mean it when I do."

Suddenly, his lips were a breath from hers. "Then you've left me no choice," he said in a silky promise. "I simply won't ever let you say goodbye." His mouth slanted over hers, a quick caress of his tongue against hers. "Now. Let's go check on Mark and Marcie—together."

Bobby grabbed her hand and led her to the door, giving her no time to object. Her mind was still reeling as they entered the hallway only to find Marcie giggling and hiccupping.

Bobby and Jennifer exchanged a look, and Bobby quickly reacted. "I'll help her," he said, scooping Marcie into his arms and carrying her toward her room.

"Bobby," Marcie groaned. "Where's Jennifer?"

"I'm here," Jennifer said, rushing through the door of the bedroom that Marcie and Mark shared, and pulling back the forest-green comforter on the bed. Bobby settled her onto the bed, and Jennifer tugged off her shoes.

Sally entered the room. "Is she okay?"

"She'll be fine," Jennifer answered. "But where is Mark? Why didn't he carry her up?"

"Mark was playing dice with Scott. He said he needed his bride and his best man to jump out of some plane with him if he was going to be properly married." She frowned. "I'm in the wedding, and I don't remember anything about a plane."

"No," Bobby said dryly. "Not you."

"Well, not the best man either because Scott said he'd rather streak naked at the twenty-four-hour grocery store than jump out of some damn plane."

Jennifer's eyes locked with Bobby's as they both had an "oh, crap" moment. "Are you telling me," Jennifer asked, "that Mark and Scott walked to the grocery store so Scott could streak?"

"Yeah," Sally said. "Them and some other guys. They're streaking all right."

Bobby sighed and scrubbed his jaw. "I'll go take care of it."

"Thank you," Jennifer said, so glad Bobby was there, the ever-steady hand in these situations, as he had been in the past. No. As they had been together. Together they'd been a good team. Her chest tightened.

Bobby nodded and turned away, Sally following, but not before Jennifer saw the shadows flicker across his face, the expression that had said *"And you wonder why I'm so afraid of becoming a drunk?"* The kind of look she'd seen from him many times and dismissed.

Guilt twisted inside Jennifer. She'd never pressed him beyond a gentle nudge to explain those looks, and she should have. She should have seen how badly he was hurting. Maybe he hadn't shut her out. Maybe he simply didn't know how to let her in.

BOBBY FOUND MARK, Scott and about five other guys gathered in the corner of the twenty-four-hour grocery store parking lot roughly three miles from the house and not a minute too soon. Scott was stripping off his clothes and was already down to bare feet and a bare chest.

With a quick turn of the wheel, Bobby pulled to the center of the circle the men had formed and shoved open his door. "Party's over, guys."

"Bobby!" Mark called out, holding up his open beer. "Thanks for the seat." He hopped onto the hood of the car. "We were looking for you. Can you believe Scott is such a pansy, he would rather run buck naked through the parking lot than skydive. The little crybaby."

"Get dressed, Scott," Bobby said, snatching his shirt and tossing it at him. "We're going home." Bobby eyed Mark. "Where your wife-to-be is waiting on you."

"I will be home to my woman just as soon as I get a picture of this," he said, snatching his cell phone and getting it camera ready.

"Oh, nasty," another guy Bobby didn't know said. "No naked pictures of Scott."

Another guy added an exaggerated, alcohol-induced laugh, and said, "Scott's gonna make all the people in the store cry when they see his shiny white ass."

Several others chanted. "Streak. Streak. Streak."

"Get dressed," Bobby ordered Scott, who was gulping a beer someone handed him.

"Get naked!" Scott yelled and down went his pants and underwear. He kicked them away from his already bare feet, and then he was running, or rather streaking.

Oh, hell. Bobby grimaced. Sirens sounded. Oh, double bloody hell. Bobby had seen plenty of drunk soldiers, but they knew when and where to drink, and how to stay out of trouble. At least, at the level of operation Bobby functioned in.

The entire group was freaking out. Except Mark who was more dazed and confused, with a big "grin before I pass out" look on his face.

Bobby quickly grabbed Mark's beer, set it down and half hoisted him into the car. "You stay here and say nothing."

Mark smiled. "Okay." His head fell backward, against the seat. Well. At least, Mark was out of the picture. Or so he hoped. He could imagine the wrath of Marcie and Jennifer if he let the groom get arrested tonight.

Bobby eyed the cop handcuffing Scott, and wasn't so sure he could save the best man but he had to try. He drew a breath and headed toward the scene of the crime.

One of the two cops, fifty-something and fit, with a buzz cut read like ex-military. Bobby showed him his military ID.

"You home to drink yourself into trouble, son, or what?" the cop asked Bobby.

"No, sir," Bobby assured him. "In fact, I haven't had even a sip of anything tonight. One of my close friends is getting married and I promised to keep her fiancé out of trouble. It appears I'm failing miserably."

The cop arched a brow. "Bachelor party?" Bobby nodded. Then the cop asked, "The streaker's the groom?"

"The best man," Bobby said. "The groom's in my car and smart enough to stay there and let me handle it. And I have to tell you, I feel to blame. I dared them all to skydive, and the best man said he'd rather streak than jump out of a plane. I turned my back a few minutes, and they were gone."

The cop chuckled. "Amazing how the idea of jumping from ten thousand feet will make a man get naked and stupid," he said, "when half the military is begging to get airborne and these civilians are scared to jump."

"I'd say a few beers added to the naked and stupid problem. Which was why everyone's keys were kept at the door. But they walked."

"You made everyone leave their keys at the door?"

"The groom did," Bobby said. "He's a good guy. Even made the guests leave cab fare at the door. He was prepared."

"Well, then," the cop said. "That is admirable." He studied Bobby. "How long you been in the Army, son?"

"Seven years," Bobby said. "Five in Special Forces."

"I was in fifteen," the cop said. "First Cavalier down in Fort Hood. Where you stationed?"

"Depends what day of the week you ask me," Bobby said, accepting his ID back and slipping it in his wallet.

"Is there a woman behind the pain I felt in those words?"

"What makes you think there's a woman?"

"There's always a woman, son," he said. "That's why I got out. I didn't want her getting cold at night and finding someone else to warm her up." He eyed the other officer talking to Scott, whose bare backside was staring them in the face, the rest of the guys all sitting on a curb where they'd been ordered. He glanced back at Bobby. "Now, I go home after a night of scary bare butts and hug my wife."

"And?" Bobby asked. "Are you happy?"

"You take the good with the bad, the bare butts with the bank robbers. I'll load these guys up and follow you to the party—after I scare the living shit out of them so they don't do this stupid crap again. But you keep them out of trouble the rest of the night."

The cop turned away, not giving Bobby a chance to thank him. Bobby realized right then, he had to figure out what he would do with himself outside the Army. He had to have an identity, a plan. He had to figure out who he was if not a soldier. Hard to do when his orders, to check out this Rocky guy and his Texas Hotzone skydiving operation, meant incorporating duty into the wedding event. Bobby scrubbed his jaw. One thing was for sure, he wasn't going to chase bare butts or bank robbers. But neither was he letting anyone else warm Jennifer's bed.

THREE HOURS AFTER Jennifer discovered Marcie in the hallway, Marcie finally slept, and Jennifer rested in the overstuffed chair in the corner. Bobby had long ago brought Mark, Scott and several other members of the wedding party back, after barely saving them from the police. Since then, the party had cleared, and Mark was passed out on the couch where Bobby had left him.

Jennifer curled her legs in the chair, and rested her head on the cushion when a shiver of awareness washed over her at the sound of footsteps approaching, the sounds of Bobby's loose-legged swagger, impossible to miss. Jennifer looked up as he appeared in the doorway.

"How's Marcie?" he asked, leaning on the door frame.

"She's okay, but she'll have a rotten hangover tomorrow," Jennifer said. "I guess fun comes with a price. At least she's resting now."

He cast her a heavy-lidded inspection. "What about you?" he asked. "Don't you need to rest?"

She rubbed the back of her neck, fighting the weariness weighing on her. "I figured I'd stay here in case she needs me. It's not like Mark can help her. He can't even get up the stairs himself."

He narrowed his gaze, his scrutiny intense, his presence seeming to swell in the room. "Not because you're trying to avoid me?"

She drew a deep breath, too tired to analyze how she felt, or why. "I'm not avoiding you, Bobby," she said softly. "You were wonderful tonight. I don't know what I would have done if you hadn't been here…to help."

His expression didn't change; he didn't move. But the silence was rich with implications, with a connection of two lovers lost, now found. Silence slid between them, weaving strands of the past with the present, alluringly warm, impossible to deny, let alone escape.

Bobby pushed off the wall and sauntered toward her. Her heart thundered in her ears, her body thrummed with anticipation of the moment he would speak, the instant he would touch her. He stopped beside the chair, towering over her.

"You're not avoiding me?" he asked again.

She shook her head, barely finding her voice. "No. I'm not avoiding you."

"Then you won't mind if I stay right here with you," he said, sitting down in the oversize chair with her and maneuvering her under his arm, against his chest.

Jennifer relaxed into Bobby, his strong arms and body warming her inside and out. She was too tired to fight the intimacy, too tired to keep her walls up, to protect herself from getting hurt again. Jennifer rested her head on his chest and let her eyes slide shut, vowing to get things back on track and all about sex tomorrow.

9

JENNIFER'S CELL PHONE RANG on the nightstand by Marcie's bed, and Jennifer jerked to a sitting position. She blinked awake and the sound of the phone jangling faded into a distant thrum as she found herself staring into Bobby's deep blue eyes. Awareness rushed through her as she remembered lying down on his chest; she had been sleeping in his arms, was still in his arms.

"Oh, God," Marcie moaned. "Make it stop." She knocked over a glass on the nightstand trying to find Jennifer's phone. "Please have mercy. Please. Make it stop!"

Jennifer shook herself into action, pushing out of Bobby's arms, and snagging the phone just as it stopped ringing.

Marcie leaned up and cast the 8:00 a.m. time on the clock a disapproving glance. She dropped to her back, covering her face with her hands. "Please tell me that call was necessary."

"It's my service," Jennifer said and punched the re-dial button. "They wouldn't call unless a patient had an emergency. So yes. It's necessary." She'd arranged to open the clinic late that afternoon for a few hours.

After talking to her service, Jennifer called her client, only to find out that her patient, a poodle, had eaten a bag of chocolates, and was sick.

"How soon can you be at the office?" Jennifer asked the poodle's owner, glancing at Bobby, who was watching her intently.

As her client responded, Jennifer turned away from Bobby, surprised to hear how far the customer drove to see her, but pleased when she was told it was because she was trusted.

Jennifer glanced at the clock. "Then nine-thirty? Does that work?"

With the time set, Jennifer hung up the line, Bobby's gaze catching hers, his expression unreadable, but warm, like those strong arms holding her only minutes before.

"I'm going in your closet, Marcie," Jennifer said. "I don't have time to go home and shower and still make it to the clinic."

"If you will stop talking so loudly," Marcie murmured, "I will give you my entire closet. Actually please stop talking. Please take what you need and leave."

Bobby smiled and stood up. "I'll take that as a cue to go check on Mark."

Forty-five minutes later, Jennifer stood in Marcie's kitchen surrounded by the aftermath of the party, a mess of trash, cups and food everywhere. Jennifer had showered and dressed, though her options had been limited considering Marcie dwarfed her by three inches and all her pants were too long. She'd settled on a simple black shell dress, bare legs and heels that thankfully fit.

Jennifer poured coffee in a mug and set it in front of Marcie, who sat at the bar, her pale faced smudged with dark circles under her eyes.

"Thank you," Marcie said grumpily, and not all so convincingly.

"I didn't make the coffee for you," Jennifer said. "I made it for everyone who has to tolerate you while hungover. I'm headed to the clinic so thankfully I'm not included in that group."

Marcie scoffed and shoved a clump of unruly hair from her eyes. She truly looked like death warmed over. "Oh, please. You're no better than me without your coffee. And I loaned you clothes. You should be nice to me." She started to sip her coffee and stopped to add, "And I'm the bride. That's a free ticket to tolerance, even if I admitted that I only had decaf in the house."

Jennifer gave her a mocking smile and leaned on the counter. "Which is why I made *you* coffee, not everyone else. I was joking about that part. Sort of. A little. Not really." She blinked. "Wait. Are you telling me the coffee in that canister I used is decaf?"

"Uh-huh," Marcie said, sipping from her cup with a keen eye. "Mark felt I was jittery with the wedding approaching."

"Okay then," Jennifer said. "I'm headed to Starbucks so you can keep the thermos I was about to fill. Actually, I'll take it and put a second cup in it." She narrowed her gaze. "Be nice to your husband-to-be while I'm gone or I won't bring it back." The two lovebirds had been snapping at each other yet again this morning, and Jennifer was starting to worry about them.

"He tricked me into agreeing to skydive," Marcie

said. "And he forced decaf on me. You know how serious that is."

Bobby sauntered into the kitchen, looking weary, his eyes heavy. Jennifer had a feeling he hadn't slept at all. "Do I smell coffee?" he asked.

"It's all your fault," Marcie accused, glaring at Bobby. "You and your stupid 'let's go skydiving' suggestion. Well, Bobby, I'll tell you right now, if I'm skydiving, let's go today when I'm nice and sick so I can aim in your direction."

"Reservations are for tomorrow," he said, snagging a cup from the cabinet and filling it. "Mark and I planned it so everyone could recover from the party. And don't either of you tell me you can't go." He eyed Jennifer. "I know you close your clinic that day." His gaze shifted to Marcie. "And Mark has the bar covered." Jennifer handed him the vanilla creamer on the counter without thinking, knowing he liked it. He took it from her, a twinkle in his eyes, telling her he caught what she'd done.

"Don't get too excited," she told him. "It's decaf."

Bobby set the cream down. "Oh, hell. What the flip, Marcie? I thought only little old ladies bought decaf."

"And high-strung brides-to-be," Mark said, walking into the kitchen, looking about as half-dead as Marcie. "Drastic actions were required if I'm going to survive until the wedding."

"You want me to jump out of a plane, but I can't have caffeine," Marcie complained. "That's wrong."

Mark arched a brow. "I'm not seeing the problem." He glanced at Bobby. "Can you help me roll the cover over the dance floor, man? I don't want those guys moaning at me when they come to pick it up."

"Sure," Bobby said, without hesitation. Bobby had always been willing to help a friend. Last night had proven to Jennifer that hadn't changed. She liked that about him. One of the things that had made loving Bobby so easy was liking him. Jennifer turned away, put the thermos in the cabinet, intentionally giving Bobby her back for fear her expression was a little too transparent—the "I loved you, please don't let me love you again" feeling twisting in her stomach.

Mark walked to Marcie and kissed her. "And don't you moan at me either, or I might have to turn you over my knee."

"Promises, promises," Marcie mumbled.

Jennifer shut the cabinet to find Bobby sipping the coffee and setting it down. He winked at Jennifer. "Pretend there is caffeine. It tastes the same."

"It's the jolt, not the taste, I was going for," she assured him.

Before she knew his intention, he grabbed her and kissed her. "How's that for a jolt?" he asked softly.

She'd let him know when she stopped vibrating, which might be several hours from now. "Bobby," she chided.

He leaned close, his lips near her ear, his breath warm, his body hot and hard. "You felt good last night," he whispered.

"Ready, Bobby?" Mark asked. Bobby pulled back and gave a nod to Mark, but his gaze was on Jennifer. "I'm ready." He then pressed a tender kiss to her forehead, a boyfriend kind of kiss, not a two-week bedroom buddy kiss, and walked away.

"He's ready," Marcie said, the minute Bobby and

Mark disappeared. "Are you? Or did you get your fill last night?"

Jennifer wasn't about to have this conversation. "The only thing I'm ready for right now," she said, "is Starbucks." She glanced at her watch. "Oh." She grabbed her purse. "I need to run."

Marcie made a chicken sound. "Run is right. From Bobby."

Jennifer scoffed and started toward the door, calling over her shoulder, "Why would I run from two weeks of incredible sex?"

But deep in her heart, she knew she was, indeed, running. Running because no matter how many times she told herself sex alone was enough with Bobby, sex was a way to end this on her terms, she knew she could only take so many of Bobby's mind-blowing kisses before she got hurt. And she liked to think she was smarter than that, having learned from past mistakes. Yeah, she thought. She had learned how to get hurt by Bobby. She was highly skilled at it, in fact. So much so, that she feared she might be excelling at doing it all over again.

SIX HOURS LATER, with one emergency after the other, Jennifer's short-term caffeine rush had long ago faded, and her lack of sleep was wearing on her quickly.

"You're sure it's allergies?" said Kate Wilmore, a sixteen-year-old pet owner of Roxie, the Chihuahua panting at her feet. Kate's youthful features frayed with worry as Jennifer walked her to the door. Her father had gone to pull the car to the door.

"I'm positive," Jennifer assured her, well aware from

Kate's fears from the exam room, that she'd lost a pet several years before to pneumonia.

"We told you she snored all night," Kate said. "Right?"

"Yes," Jennifer said. "You told me. The steroid shot I gave her will work wonders, I promise. Snoring is perfectly normal with allergies."

The door to the clinic opened but instead of Kate's father, Bobby stepped inside. "You said you weren't going to tell anyone I snored."

Instant adrenaline rocketed through Jennifer, all sense of exhaustion gone, but somehow she kept her expression unaffected despite the discreet head-to-toe inspection he gave her. Kate didn't notice, she was smiling up at Bobby, her eyes lighting with teenage appreciation, and Jennifer couldn't blame her. Clean-shaven, with faded jeans, a snug Army T-shirt and his blue eyes shimmering in a backdrop of sunlight, he looked country-boy sexy.

Roxie barked and huddled at Bobby's feet. He squatted down and gave the pup a rubdown. "Hey there, cutie," he said and smiled at Kate. "Yours, I take it?"

"Yes," she said brightly, the worry from moments before fading away. "Her name is Roxie, and she snores, too."

"Really?" Bobby said. "Small world. You know, when I was in college, I had a German shepherd that snored. The two of us together drove Jennifer crazy."

"Jennifer?" Kate frowned.

Bobby pushed to his feet and eyed Jennifer, his expression lighting with pride. "Dr. Jones," he corrected.

Kate looked between them and said, "So you two are—"

"No," Jennifer said quickly.

"I'm in the doghouse right now," Bobby told Kate. "But I'm howling my way back out."

Kate laughed and the door opened as her father poked his head in. "Ready, Kate?"

"Yes," she said quickly before eying Jennifer. "Thank you, Dr. Jones."

"Call me if you need me," Jennifer said, waving.

The door shut, leaving Jennifer and Bobby alone. "You're making a habit of leaving without saying a proper goodbye," Bobby said. "You didn't even give me a phone number."

"I was in a rush to get to work," she said quickly.

"And away from me," he added, and didn't give her time to object. "So this is your clinic." He scanned the lobby—the tiled flooring, to make accidents easier to clean up; simple cloth chairs, again, easy to clean; and pictures of animals on the walls. "You did it," he said, more of that earlier pride in his voice and his face. "You made your dream come true." His voice softened. "I'm happy for you, Jen. I really am. You knew what you wanted and you went after it."

"Thank you," she said, sadness balling in her chest. It was her dream, yes, but seven years ago, she'd shared it with Bobby. Expected to live it with him. "And you? Did you find what you wanted?"

His jaw tensed in a barely perceptible way, his answer coming slowly. "Yeah," he said. "I found what I wanted."

It was all she could do not to press her hand to her stomach at the coiling inside. Good. That was good. She did want him to be happy. She did. She loved him. That meant letting go sometimes. She understood that; it was the *not* saying goodbye, *not* dealing with the past, that had been hard. She had that chance now, and she should be thankful. Right. Thankful. Embrace opportunity.

She cleared her throat. "The door," she said, trying to move beyond the moment because the embracing-opportunity thing really wasn't calling to her. "Can you lock that door behind you? Roxie was my last patient, and I don't want to risk any walk-ins without anyone covering the front."

He stared at her, his blue eyes probing hers, before he turned to the door. "Ah, Jen," he said, messing with the lock. "Is there a trick to this lock that you forgot to mention?"

Jennifer squeezed her eyes shut. "Oh, God, no," she said, weary to the bone. "I had a new door put in two weeks ago, and the lock hasn't worked right since. I just had a guy out here last week to replace it." She pressed her hand to her face and then let it fall. "I can't leave the place open. I'll have to call the locksmith."

Bobby opened the door and gave it a quick once-over, moving it back and forth. "It's not the lock. It's the door. It's off center. I can fix you right up if you have a tool kit."

"You don't have to do that, Bobby," Jennifer said. The idea of him taking care of this for her was hitting a sensitive spot. She didn't want to depend on Bobby. He was leaving. "I can call someone."

"I'm here," he said. "Why wouldn't I do this for you?"

Of course. Why wouldn't he? "Tool kit coming right up," she said.

Thirty minutes later, Bobby appeared in the doorway of her office. "All done and locked up."

Jennifer pushed to her feet. "Great. Thank you." He was so big and sexy, and her office, so small and confining. Jennifer gathered her purse from her desk, ready to escape. She wasn't going to get perspective until she slept. "I desperately need a few hours of shut-eye."

Bobby propped himself in the door frame. "The skydiving operation we're going to tomorrow...they're doing an exhibition show tonight. I was hoping, after you got a few hours' rest, of course, that maybe we could drive out there together."

Usually one to think before she acted, or spoke, Jennifer found herself unable to contain the explosiveness of her instant reaction. Her purse went down on the desk with a thud. "No, Bobby," she said. "No, we cannot drive out to the exhibition show. Just like you shouldn't have fixed my door. We," she said, waving her hand between them in an exaggerated fashion, "are not dating. We do not do dating-type things. This is a fling. Nothing but a fling. An ends-in-less-than-two-weeks fling! That translates to sex and goodbye. Goodbye and sex. We've had this conversation. You don't have to walk around that. You don't have to make it pretty." She was mad. She couldn't help it. "Just make it good!"

His expression hardened, stone-cold and calculating, in a way she'd rarely seen Bobby. He stared at her. She stared at him. And then suddenly, she said, "Darn it, Bobby, I know you're mad. But what right do you have to be mad? You left me. You were silent for seven long years. You cannot come back here and just expect me to fall at your feet. I didn't do this to us. You did."

He pierced her with a shadowy, haunted gaze. "I thought there was no 'us' to do anything to, Jen," he said. "So is there or is there not?"

"There was," she said softly, fists balled by her side as she tried to stop her hands from trembling, telling herself it was lack of sleep, when she knew it was him, it was Bobby, his nearness. The need to feel him touch her again, the fear he would and that she would lose herself to him forever this time.

"But not now?" he pressed. "Now there is only sex?"

She drew a shaky breath at the directness of the question, at the tension crackling in the air, as if the elements around them waited for an answer as surely as he did. She didn't understand him, didn't understand any of this.

"I'm not pressuring you, Bobby," she said. "I'm not asking you for forever. I didn't ask you to explain the past. You don't have to do any of this. I won't let our past ruin the wedding. But you keep pressing. I don't know what you want from me. What is it you want, Bobby?"

10

WHAT DID HE WANT FROM HER? The question hung in Jennifer's office for long seconds as Bobby drew a heavy breath, struggling to rein in his emotions. That she even had to ask him what he wanted ate him alive. But he'd been gone seven long years, home only a few days, and that gave her plenty of reason to doubt his intentions as honorable. She didn't know what he did— she didn't know he wanted to wake up next to her every morning forever more, to share the ups and downs of life with her. She didn't know Bobby wanted it all. That he'd secretly always wanted it all. He knew that now; perhaps he'd always known it.

He pressed his forehead to hers, tightness expanding in his chest. "You want to know why I'm mad?" he challenged, their breath mingling as he returned to her initial question. He could almost taste the bittersweet tang of her mouth. "I'm mad because I had you, and I was foolish enough to walk away. Because you keep pushing me away, and I know you have every right and reason. Because I want more than your body, and all I can have is sex. And I need…" Raw emotion splintered through him, creating jagged, shadowy emotions. "I need."

She slid into his arms as if she knew exactly what he needed—her.

"Bobby," she gasped, her hands curling in his shirt, the sexy sound of his name on her tongue exploding erotically into the silence of the room.

"That's it, sweetheart," he said, his fingers curving over her lush backside. "Say my name." He needed to hear it enough to last a lifetime. He gently shoved his way inside her panties and then stroked her sensitive folds. "Say it again," he whispered, his lips brushing hers.

"Bobby," she hissed into his mouth, her tongue sucking his. He could feel her responding to the darkness in him, feel her looking for answers, for some sort of completion that words and seven years wouldn't allow them. He kissed her, sliding his fingers inside her, stretching her, readying her. Moving his fingers with her as she rocked against his hand.

He nipped her lip and then picked her up, carrying her to the desk and setting her down. His zipper hissed as he opened it, and he shoved his pants to his knees. Jennifer quickly got rid of her panties. She spread her legs and scooted closer to the edge of the desk, offering herself in body, if not in heart and soul.

He ground his teeth in anticipation and slid the thick head of his erection along the slick folds of her body, probing, teasing. She stared down at the intimate view, as did he, the thrum of arousal fire in his veins. He circled the blunt head in the wet heat of her cleft and then captured her mouth with his, hot and hungry, and then pressed past the intimate folds of her body, entering her, and then driving hard and deep.

Jennifer whimpered and clung to him, wrapping her arms and legs around him. Bobby lifted her, filling his hands with her lush backside. Filling her body with the thick pulse of his erection. Their breath mingled together.

She rocked against his body, slow and sensuous, up and down, side to side; he guided her movements. But it wasn't enough, not for him, not for her. Bobby used her weight, forcing her down on his shaft—harder, faster, deeper.

Drenching him with sweet, slick heat, she clung to his shoulders, her breasts pressed to his, ravishing him with sweet curves and soft moans. Again and again, he pulled her down his shaft, until she arched her back and hips, a sound of pleasure sliding from her lips just as she spasmed around him.

Bobby moaned with the intensity of her muscles milking him, dragging him to a dark, blissful place where there was only the shudder of her body against his. The shadows of the past were velvety rich with the present. There was only here, now, the two of them. He buried himself in the depths of her orgasm, buried the anger and regret eating him alive. Let the molten heat licking at his cock melt him farther inside Jennifer, clinging to every last second of the escape until he shook with the effort, unable to hold back. In an instant, Bobby's orgasm was ripped from the base of his cock, spilling himself into the depths of her body. Bobby buried his face in her jasmine-scented, silky blond hair. Tormented by the pleasure that was both perfection and hell—the pleasure that would force him back into the present. For long seconds, Bobby held her, she held him. Weakness overcame his legs, and he set her on the desk and pressed his forehead to hers. There was so much he wanted to say, so much he should say, but also, so much he wasn't sure he should say. As she had said, he had no right to come back here and expect more from her than what she was giving him.

Her hand gently rested on his jaw, the anger and demand between them absent, fading away. There was comfort in her tender touch, a sense of understanding that said she felt the vulnerability in him, the rawness of the confession he had yet to make, but he knew, stay or go, he owed her.

He swallowed what felt like a brick in his throat. "Since the Hotzone in San Marcus, we'll already be halfway to my father's place in San Antonio when the air show ends. It'll be late, so we'll want to find a hotel tonight and see him tomorrow, but I thought…I wanted, no…I need you to go with me to see *him*."

Jennifer leaned back, searching his face, surprise glinting in the depths of her blue eyes. Her gaze sharpened and then narrowed. "You haven't seen him, have you? Not since you left."

His lips thinned and he shook his head. "No," he managed to say, his throat as parched as the Iraqi desert.

Shock washed over her face. "Have you talked?"

"A couple times on the phone," he said, pulling out of her and fixing his pants while she righted her clothing and then leaned back against the desk.

"And?" she asked. "How were the talks?"

A bitter laugh slid from his throat. "You don't talk to my father," he said. "He talks. You listen."

"That good, huh?" she asked softly.

He shrugged. "It is what it is, but I left here because of him." He ground his teeth. "No. That's not true. I left because of me. Because I let him get into my head. And, Jen—" he scrubbed his jaw, the roughness of the stubble scraping against his palm "—I won't lie. He's still there. Working me over. I don't have any right to ask you to go with me. I don't have any right to ask anything of you. But I need you to know why I left, no matter how poor the decision. I need you to know it wasn't about you. Or rather—it was about you. About protecting you."

"You barely even drink, Bobby," she reminded him. "You aren't your father."

"Yeah, well," Bobby said, "he was sober until he turned forty. From there, it was one big slosh fest. Still is from what I can tell from a distance."

She pushed off the desk, a solemn look on her heart-shaped face as she stopped in front of him. Her hands pressed to his chest, heating the area she touched. She blinked up at him. "You really believe you're going to turn into him, don't you?"

"No," he answered honestly. "I wouldn't be here now if I hadn't come to realize I'm not my father. That my choices, just like his did, will decide my future. But deep down, I know I'm kidding myself if I believe I've dealt with this, not until I go and face him."

She studied. "I wish I would have seen this in you before. I wish I…"

He pulled her close and kissed her. "Stop. Do not even think about making what happened somehow your fault. You do that—you take things on as your own. You didn't see this in me, because I'm not sure I did. I hid from it. I've been hiding from it for seven years. I'm here now. It's time I face him, and myself." His gaze brushed her parted lips, wet from their kisses, the sweetness that was so her, without her even trying. "I was young and scared, Jen. I was running. It's all I knew how to do."

"From me," she murmured. "You ran from me."

"I ran from myself," he said, cupping her cheek. "Not you. And I'm not running now. I'm laying it all on the line here. Everything I am."

Turbulence flickered across her face. Slowly, she nodded. "Let's go see your father. Get it over with now. Get this behind you."

Bobby stood there, basking in the acceptance in her eyes, in the willingness to be there for him he didn't deserve, when he'd deserted her.

Drowning. Bobby was drowning in a deep pool of water that felt as if it might turn into some of that quicksand he'd experienced back in that Iraqi desert. Jennifer was going with him to see his father. It was what he'd wanted. So why did he have a knot fisted in his gut? Because, he knew, he was afraid of pulling Jen into the quicksand with him.

He lifted her hand, pressed her fingers to his mouth. "Go home and rest," he finally said. "You'll need it to deal with my father. I'll need it to deal with my father."

"Then come with me," she said. "We'll sleep a few hours and leave from my place."

"If I come home with you…" he said in a thick tone, thinking of how good stripping her naked and holding her would be, "I won't let you sleep."

"Sleep is overrated," she said. "Come home with me, Bobby."

But that tight feeling in his chest was back. He had

to figure out how to dig himself out of this quicksand. "I've got stuff going on in my head," he said. "I need to deal with it." He touched her cheek. "I'll pick you up at seven, okay?"

Confusion slid across her face. "Okay," she reluctantly agreed.

His hands settled on her shoulders. "Thank you for coming with me, Jen." He kissed her forehead and turned to leave, telling himself he was headed back to the hotel to review the encrypted files being sent to him on the Texas Hotzone skydiving operation and its owner. Telling himself he had duty. Work. Preparation for an assignment that might well be his last, but one he wanted to complete. He'd seen plenty of guys exit the Army and struggle in the civilian world. Hell, he could be one of those guys. He wouldn't convict one of his own, a fellow soldier, without doing what he could to save him.

It was easier to focus on that than the questions Jennifer would ask if he stayed with her—about his mind-set now, about his mind-set seven years ago. He couldn't talk about his father. Not with Jennifer. Not without backing out of this visit. Because Bobby might be prepared to face the past, to face his father and himself, but was she? And was he really being fair to ask her to?

Maybe he'd been selfish to return home, to pull her into this. But he had. He'd not only returned home, he'd tasted her, held her, felt the sweetness of her presence surround him. And Lord help him, he felt selfish. Because he wanted more of her.

Deep down, though, he feared she would not want more than their "fling," as she called it. He feared he'd pushed her away, pushed her too far, for too long, and she really was simply saying goodbye. That he'd lost her, and no matter how hard he tried to win her back, he could not.

He wasn't sure he was the man who could make her happy. Or maybe he could. By giving her a chance to say goodbye. He needed her to have that choice. Exactly why he wasn't going to tell her about his reenlistment. He wasn't going to put that kind of pressure on her. If she needed to use him and throw him aside, if revenge was all she needed from him, he'd give it to her. But not without trying to convince her forever had a place—with him.

_11_

WITH BOBBY DUE to pick her up any minute, Jennifer scanned her appearance in the solid oak, full-length mirror in the corner of her bedroom. After far too much debate, she wore her black jeans again and a black tee, the V-neck lined with a tiny strand of delicate silver sequins—not overdone, just a tiny bit of feminine accent. Black boots completed the outfit, preparation for being on who-knew-what terrain for the air show. Freshly washed, her hair fell in silky waves on her shoulders, but would most likely be a frizzy mess once she stepped into the Texas August heat. But then, so would everyone else's—at least it'd look good for when she opened the door and saw Bobby again. If only she'd actually slept and didn't have dark circles smudged beneath ineffective makeup.

When Jennifer would have turned away, her gaze lingered on the mirror, not at her own image, but on the antique wood, and the history it represented. It had been her grandmother's. As had the chest-high jewelry box beside it. She'd filled her little condo with the warmth of family, with furniture and trinkets, photos and memories. But Bobby had none of those things. He only had his father, who wasn't much of a father at all, it seemed.

"He has you," she whispered to the image in the mirror. She'd already made that decision, while lying in bed not sleeping and wondering what Bobby had going on in his head right now. Knowing he needed her and she'd be there for him, no strings attached. Oh, sure, he seemed to want her now, but after hearing about his father, she knew that feeling stemmed from his need to broach the past. She understood she was a part of his healing. She certainly believed he was a part of her healing. No matter how this ended, she had her closure. And she knew now, she'd needed closure desperately.

The doorbell rang and Jennifer's heart raced wildly at the sound. She was nervous. With Bobby. As if they hadn't seen each other in every intimate way possible. As if they hadn't just had sex several hours before. As if this was a date.

"It's not a date," she said softly, rushing toward the door. He was leaving. Again. This was a fling with hot sex and a final kiss goodbye—the end that should have happened before, and never did. A bit of entertainment outside the bedroom was not so abnormal. But Bobby... at her door, knocking when he'd once had a key to her home and her heart, this felt abnormal.

She reached for the doorknob and inhaled a calming breath before pulling it open. "Hi," she said, bringing him into focus, her calming breath lodging in her throat, and not so calming after all.

Bobby leaned on the door frame, one powerful arm looped over his head, his big, gorgeous body filling the archway. The scent of him inviting her body's response.

"Hi," he said softly, while his eyes screamed with crystal-blue awareness.

Jennifer pulled the door open fully. "Come in and I'll get my purse from the bedroom."

He dropped his arm and sauntered forward, pushing the door shut behind him. Before she knew his intention, he tugged her into his arms. His lips brushed hers, a caress, a promise, though of what she did not know. "Did you rest?" he asked.

"I tried and failed," she admitted, her hand brushing his cheek as she noted the weariness beneath the sex appeal. "You didn't rest either, did you?"

"Rest is overrated, right?" he teased, his hand lazily caressing her back, sending shivers down her spine as he reminded her of her earlier comment. "Guess we could have spent the afternoon in bed after all." He molded her closer. "We might have time—"

She pressed away from him. "Or we might lose track of time and forget the show. And for the record, this show is the closest you are getting me to a parachute."

"You forget how persuasive I can be," he reminded her, nuzzling her ear. "Should I remind you?" His hands slid up her waist, brushing the curves of her breasts.

Jennifer sucked in a breath as her nipples tingled and tightened, and she pulled back to glower at him. "Have you forgotten how stubborn I can be? Should *I* remind *you?*"

"I've definitely not forgotten how stubborn you are," he teased in an exaggerated voice and swatted her backside. "You win the battle of wills." He winked. "For now. Go get your purse and let's roll. The show's in San

Marcus at the actual Texas Hotzone airfield where we'll be jumping tomorrow."

"Not we," she corrected. "I already told you. I'm not jumping out of any airplane. And don't try to change my mind. Tell me about the show instead. Is it some sort of festival or charity type thing or what?"

"Someone at the Hotzone told me about it when I called to book the reservations," he said. "They put the show on themselves once a month to draw interest and new customers. We just got lucky with the timing." He glanced at his watch. "Show starts in forty-five minutes. It's about a thirty-minute drive, if I remember my distances correctly."

"We should have taken Marcie and Mark," she suggested, and then realized her error. They were going to see his father in San Antonio. He wouldn't want Mark and Marcie along for the ride. She crinkled her nose. "Then again, it might have started a fight we don't want to be a part of."

Bobby kissed her forehead, appearing unaffected by her misstep. "I wanted to have you all to myself anyway."

The confession vibrated with a sweet, romantic kind of sensuality that made her smile. "I can live with that," she admitted, and then, with an undeniable smile inside to match the one outside, Jennifer whisked away to her bedroom. She returned a few seconds later, ready to leave. "Should we take my car?"

He dangled a key in his hand and wiggled an eyebrow. "We're riding in style, sweetheart. An Infiniti G Series." He held the door open. "And it's a convertible."

"That's a pricy rental there, soldier," she said, flipping off the lights as she stepped outside.

"Just call me Sugar Daddy," he joked and kissed her. He took her keys, as if it were second nature, and locked the door, as he explained, "Free upgrade. They lost my reservations and I had to wait an hour."

"Still got a pickup at home?" she asked, as they walked to the parking lot to the right of her condo.

He stiffened, a barely perceivable shift in his body, but she didn't miss it. "If you mean at the base," he said, holding the door of the shiny silver Infiniti open for her as she slid inside. "A white F150." He didn't give her time to respond, shutting her inside the car, where the scent of new leather threaded through her nostrils, sadness in her chest.

He claimed the driver's seat and started the engine, sudden tension palpable. Jennifer glanced at his profile, noting the hard set to his jaw. "I didn't mean to imply this isn't your home," she said softly. "I… Well, you've been gone seven years."

"You didn't say anything wrong," he said, maneuvering out of the parking space. "This isn't my home. It hasn't been for a long time. Hell. I don't know why I have a truck back at base. I'm deployed more often than not. I'm rarely even in the same country where it's parked, let alone driving it."

"You're gone that much?"

He nodded. "My unit is small and specialized," he said. "We don't technically exist. Top secret, done off the grid that no one else will touch. It's not exactly a situation cut out for home and family. In fact, one of our members just opted out of reenlistment after meeting a woman he wanted to marry. He didn't want to put her through the hell of the life we lead. And it was the right decision. He almost got himself killed on his final mission. He was distracted. Survival in our unit means treating our duty, and nothing else, as our home. Lives depend on it."

The butterflies were back in Jennifer's stomach, but this time, they felt more like bats, clawing her inside out. "And does it?" she asked softly. "Feel like home?"

Seconds ticked by before he replied in a low, gravelly voice, his attention latched on to the road, "It's been the only home I've had for seven years."

Jennifer tore her gaze from his profile, and stared out of the window, the sun lowering rapidly into a skyline blended with blues, yellows and oranges. He was leaving. She'd known this, but maybe on some level, she'd prayed it wasn't true despite telling herself she was ready for closure, ready for goodbye. Prayed that there could still be something between them beyond the past.

But he was married to duty; duty was home. The only part of the past that could exist was goodbye. That should be liberating. The pressure was off. The fling was on. Closure could be found without turmoil. It was liberating. It was everything she should want. So why wasn't she relieved?

AS SOON AS THEY HIT highway I-35 driving toward San Marcus, Bobby gently nudged Jennifer into talking about her clinic. Fortunately, once the topic of her animals was rolling, Jennifer was quick to forget about his past, or future, in the Army. And the more she talked, the more he realized what a good life she'd made for herself. The more he knew that his decision to keep his enlistment status a secret was the right one. Somehow, some way, when these two weeks ended, she was going to be happy, with or without him. Without guilt, without regret. Hopefully without throwing things, because that would mean he'd gone terribly wrong somewhere along the line.

Arriving at the show grounds, Bobby's one regret was the need to detour from his plan to bury the ghost of the past, for an investigative operation. They parked behind one of two large warehouses, overlooking an airfield.

Well-populated steel bleachers were set up on the building side of the airfield. Not far from the seating, smoke floated from several oversize barbecue grills near a large concession stand.

Jennifer stepped out of the car as Bobby held the door open. She inhaled. "Oh, that smells good," she said and pressed her hand to her stomach. "I'm hungry."

He laughed. "For a little thing, you've always had the appetite of a linebacker."

She shoved her hands on her hips. "Your point?"

"Other than I like that you actually eat and don't pick…" he said, taking her hand and leading her toward where they had to register. He was about to get his first look at Rocky Smith and his Hotzone skydiving operation, that might well be a cover for running illegal drugs to and from Mexico. "No point at all."

"I think the point should really be—you need to feed me sometime soon," she argued.

"Just like old times." He laughed, remembering eating out with Jennifer at their favorite spots. The little Mexican place on Lamar Boulevard, the cafeteria on Research Avenue. The Chinese place next door to it. "I promise to feed you as soon as we get our tickets and our seats."

"I'll go grab us some food while you register, so we don't miss the show," she suggested.

He reached for his pocket to give her money. She sidled up to him, her hands on his hips, body pressed close. "I don't want your money," she said. "You buy the show tickets. I can cover the cost of the food."

His hand slid up her back. "I invited you, Jen."

"Save the macho routine for the bedroom," she chided. "Or wherever else we might…enjoy one another. But if you try to give me your money, I reserve the right to punch you, and I most certainly will."

"Wasn't it 'throw' something at me?" he asked.

"If you prefer," she said agreeably. She gave him a short, no less alluring, kiss, before turning on her heels, and then sashayed her cute little curvy ass toward the barbecue pits. Bobby's gaze lingered on her a moment before he laughed and shook his head, heading into the building.

A shot of instant, cool air rushed over him as he stepped into the tiled lobby of the facility, a long, counter-style, built-in desk as the centerpiece. Behind it, several desks and file cabinets scattered an open bull-pen setting. A few last-minute ticket buyers crowded the thirty-something brunette behind the counter.

Bobby held back, watching and listening, patiently making use of the wait to evaluate the operation.

The phone rang and a man dressed in a burnt-orange flight suit appeared from somewhere in the back and snagged the line. A second later, the man shouted, "I need Rocky, Shari!"

The brunette eyed him over her shoulder. "Join the club," she said. "And do I look like the man's keeper?"

"There won't be any show to sell tickets to if we don't find him," the man blasted back.

One of the customers piped up at that. "No show?!"

The brunette grimaced. "Ignore him," she said. "He dramatizes when he wants attention." Then over her shoulder again. "He's in Zone 2 with Rick."

"What?" the man said. "Rick should be in the air by now!"

The woman waved him off and handed a customer tickets. "Better get a seat. The show's about to start."

Bobby advanced farther into the lobby, his mind racing with options that would allow him to pursue the man in the flight suit to Zone 2 before he was out of sight, impossible to locate.

He slid money onto the counter. "I'll take two tickets," he said. "Don't suppose there's a restroom I can use?"

The woman snatched the money without looking up. "Outhouse is in the parking lot—"

"I have reservations tomorrow," he said. "For four."

Her gaze lifted and lingered on Bobby. "Far right corner behind me, but make it snappy."

Bobby rounded the counter with a murmured "thank you," in pursuit of Zone 2, when he should have been outside with Jennifer. Where he really wanted to be. Proof that it was all or nothing with Jennifer. He was in the Army, or he was out, in her life, or out. Considering he was leaving her to fend for herself, and was forbidden from explaining his mission to her, even if he wasn't worried it would put her at risk, he had a feeling he was going to be out. Bobby was doing a good job of staying in the doghouse, instead of finding a way to make sure that Jennifer knew the Army wasn't home— she was "home."

12

BOBBY REACHED THE rear of the building and the door that said Men and kept walking straight to the exit sign. He slipped out the back. Nothing but unlit dirt landscape separated the two buildings and several airplane hangars.

The shadowy figure of the man he was following stalked toward the hangar Bobby assumed to be Zone 2. Bobby flattened himself against the wall, patiently waiting for the right time to pursue but avoid notice. The instant the man disappeared into the hangar, Bobby was on the move, closing the distance with practiced, stealthy speed.

Angry male voices lifted in the air as Bobby approached the open back doors. As he had before, he flattened himself against the wall, and then listened.

"Look, Rocky," a familiar male voice said. Bobby recognized it as belonging to the man he was following.

"Look, my ass, Gavin," Rocky growled, as Bobby inched around the corner to bring the two men, both in flight suits, into view. Rocky, who Bobby knew to be thirty-four and two years a civilian, was still in battle-ready physical condition, clean-shaven, his jaw set tight. He had something in his hand by his side, as he continued, "You adjusted the odometer on the plane. Why?"

"I don't know what you're talking about," Gavin said. "This is ridiculous. We have a show about to start."

Rocky tossed a bag of white powder onto the ground between him and Gavin. "And one of my planes was about to go up for that show with fucking cocaine inside. Explain that, Gavin. And don't feed me a line of crap. In fact…I don't want an explanation. I get that you're a lowlife piece of shit. So get off my property and do it now."

Bobby officially knew where Rocky stood. He was clean in all of this. Thank the Lord above, because that made things easier for Bobby. After he reported, his duty was done. Gavin would be placed under surveillance but he was unlikely to lead them anywhere but to another contact to monitor, who might be of interest.

"You've got this all wrong, Rocky," Gavin insisted.

"You messed with the wrong man's operation, Gavin," Rocky ground out in obvious anger, his words whiplash sharp. "I'm doing you a favor, letting you walk, because you saved my life in Iraq. But we're even now. If I see you again—"

"You don't know what you're asking," Gavin said.

"There's no asking about this, Gavin," Rocky assured him. "Get the hell out of here before I have you removed."

"I'm not going anywhere," Gavin said, his voice thickening with rebellion. "The men I work for like what I'm doing. They won't want it to end. I'll arrange compensation on your behalf."

"You have thirty seconds to get out of here," Rocky

said. "Or I *will* call the police. My debt of gratitude extends only so far."

Gavin glared. "You'll be sorry," he said. "They'll make you pay. They'll destroy you."

"Let them try," Rocky ground out.

Gavin laughed bitterly. "You are so going to regret this. I'll be back, and sooner rather than later." He stormed toward the exit, and Bobby slipped quickly to the side of the building, waiting until the right time to head back to Jennifer's side. He was relieved to know that the part of the investigation which involved the Texas Hotzone and Bobby himself was most likely over. By tomorrow, Bobby would be free to focus on Jennifer.

JENNIFER ORDERED two sausage wraps and a large Coke for her and Bobby to share, as they had in the past. Then she realized how assumptive that was and quickly adjusted. "Make that two Cokes." But how was she going to carry them? "No. Never mind. Stick with the one large."

Behind the grill, the fifty-something cowboy, with a round belly, arched one grayish-black brow. "One large? You sure?"

"Of course I'm sure," she said. "It's not like a Coke is a big decision." The cowboy's brow arched up a bit more, as if he didn't believe her.

Jennifer pursed her lips. "One large."

He chuckled and turned away. "What's so funny?" Jennifer asked, frowning.

"I've been married twenty years," the cowboy said, filling a cup from a portable drink machine to the right of the grill. "Young people dating tend to amuse me."

"I'm not on a date," Jennifer said quickly.

The cowboy chuckled again. "Of course you aren't."

"I was worried about my hands being full."

He offered her the drink. "Of course you were." With a nod, he indicated a small portable table. "Fixin's for the sandwiches, over there. Show's about to start, so you better make those links tasty quick." He grinned. "Good luck with that drink."

Jennifer bit back another denial, heat flooding her cheeks, as she turned to the "fixin's." A few minutes later she stood outside the building waiting on Bobby, wondering what was taking so long, especially considering the planes were lining up on the runway. The crowd was cheering; the show was about to begin.

Jennifer decided it was time to go find Bobby. She marched toward the door when the bag broke open, the sandwiches hitting the ground.

"Oh, no, it didn't," Jennifer murmured, bending down to try to pick up the mess and cringing. The sausages had dirt all over them. It was a mess.

Fortunately, Jennifer eyed the large metal trash can she just happened to be standing next to—which considering the smell, in hindsight, might not have been the brightest move, until now, when she needed said trash can.

She set the drink down and started to gather up the ruined sandwiches when the soda tumbled over, followed by Jennifer, as she lost her balance. She hit the wall; her butt, the dirt. "Oh, good grief," she murmured. She'd never been so clumsy in her life. First she fell in chocolate mousse, now this.

Jennifer maneuvered to get up when she heard a male

voice. "You heard me, B.J., cut one of the chutes. Eduardo wants Rocky taught a lesson." Silence a moment, as if he were listening. "B.J.," the man said in a harsh whisper, "someone has to die. Now, it can be you or me, or it can be one of those jumpers today. Decide." Another listening pause and then, "I knew you'd see it my way. Make it happen. I'll make sure Eduardo knows how helpful you were."

The air lodged in Jennifer's throat, every muscle in her body freezing with it, mentally shrinking herself to pea-size in hopes of not being seen. Surely, she'd heard wrong. Gravel crunched on the ground, the man's footsteps fading. The door opened to the building, and she prayed for Bobby, but it wasn't him.

Jennifer shoved to her feet and forgot the bag and drink. She ran for the door and grabbed it before it shut, bursting inside.

BOBBY SLIPPED IN the back door of the ticket office and rounded the corner at the same moment Jennifer appeared in the lobby and shouted, "Stop the show! Please. Stop the show."

Holy shit. He had no idea what was going on, but he wasn't going to wait to find out. Charging forward, he was at the counter by the time she said, "A chute isn't going to open. I know a chute isn't going to open."

The brunette behind the counter, the only person left in the office, shook her head. "I promise you, ma'am," she said to Jennifer, "the chutes will open. Please. Go enjoy the show."

"Jennifer!" Bobby called. "What's going on?"

She rushed to meet him as he rounded the reception counter. "Bobby. Bobby, thank God. You have to convince them to stop the show." She fumbled for her purse. "My phone. I'll call the police. Bobby, I heard—"

He kissed her, not about to allow her to involve herself as a witness in any of this, not with a drug lord involved. "Tell me outside," he whispered urgently against her lips, grabbing her hand.

"Sorry," he said to the receptionist. "She's afraid of skydiving. I shouldn't have brought her."

"Good grief," the woman scoffed. "Usually the dramatics come from the ones jumping, not the ones watching."

"Bobby!"

Adrenaline pumping, Bobby tugged her out the door. The minute he turned to face her, she shoved him. "Hey! Why did you do that?" Her fingers curled in his shirt. "I heard a man on the phone planning an accident for one of the parachuters. We have to do something."

Bobby's hands settled on her shoulders. He wanted her nowhere near any of this. "Who said what to whom?"

"A man on the phone," Jennifer said. "He told someone named B.J. to cut one of the chutes. That Rocky needed a lesson." She paused. "If they won't stop those jumps, we have to call the police!"

"Listen to me," he said. "There are things going on here I don't want you associated with. You heard nothing. I did. I heard it, and I'll deal with it. Understand?"

"But—"

"No buts," he said. "Do as I say so I can go save a life and not worry about yours. Agreed?"

"I…" She hesitated. "Fine. I heard nothing."

That worked. He wanted details, but he didn't have

time to demand more. Not when seconds could mean lives. He was already speaking to the receptionist before the door could shut behind him. "Do you have an employee named B.J.?"

"Who wants to know?"

"Sergeant Bobby Evans, Special Forces," he said, leaning across the desk. "Do you have an employee named B.J.?"

A confounded look slid over the woman's face. "Has B.J. done something wrong?"

Confirmation B.J. worked here. Enough validation to believe Jennifer had nailed the conversation she'd overheard. "Ground the planes. Call off the show."

"Sergeant Evans," came the dark bark of male command, "if you have questions about my operation, direct them to me." It was Rocky. "What seems to be the problem?"

"B.J. is involved with planning an accident during the show. Ground the planes and ground them now."

Rocky assessed him for all of two hard, icy seconds, then, "Call the planes now, Shari. Ground them."

"But, Rocky—" she started to argue.

"Do it, Shari!" Rocky insisted, moving to stand behind her. "Do it now! I'm going to the hangar. Call me with confirmation."

Jennifer burst through the door. "Bobby! The planes are lined up to taxi!"

"Shit!" Rocky and Bobby said at the same moment.

Rocky started running for the back door. Bobby turned to Jennifer. "Stay here."

Shari grabbed the radio next to the desk. "Wheels

on the ground," she ordered. "I repeat, wheels remain on the ground. Respond with confirmation."

In a matter of seconds, Bobby joined Rocky at a distant hangar, drawing up short when he heard the sound of gravel and dirt behind him. The two men drew to a halt.

"What the hell," Rocky said, hands on his hips as he looked behind them.

Bobby turned to find Jennifer running toward him, and added his own curse to the mix.

Rushing to meet her, Bobby kicked himself for bringing her here today. Shackling Jennifer's arm, he pulled her close, angry at her for not listening. Angry at himself for putting her in danger. "Damn it, woman. I told you—"

"Something is wrong with the radios," she panted. "We can't make contact, Bobby. Someone is going to jump out of that plane without a working parachute. Someone is going to die. We have to do something."

The roar of engines sounded as a plane took off. "No!" Jennifer yelled, gaping at the sky.

Bobby turned to the sky as the second took off, silently cursing.

Frantically, Jennifer repeated, "We have to do something!"

Bobby framed her face with his hands. "Baby, I am. Trust me. This is what I do. I deal with danger all the time. But I need to know you are safe. That man you heard talking—he's mixed up with some dangerous people." He pulled the car keys from his pocket and put them in her hand. "Get in the car and lock the doors. Hell. Get in the car and drive away from here."

Rocky rushed up on them, already talking. "We got

a problem," he said. "The guy I fired tonight, the one who most likely made that call to B.J., he's in the office 'helping' Shari, and I can't tell Shari he's dangerous. Not without putting her at risk." He narrowed his gaze on Bobby. "Exactly who are you and what resources do you have at your disposal?"

Bobby answered cautiously, aware of Jennifer standing with them. He grabbed the Army phone he was carrying. "Special Forces, and I do have resources. I'll have Gavin dealt with. But right now, at this very moment, considering the time we have to act…we need up in the air. You got a plane and a pilot?"

"I got both," Rocky said. "What do you have in mind?"

"Once those divers jump, our chances of saving them are next to zero. We need to be in the air, signaling them any damn way we can manage."

"What are we waiting for?" Rocky asked.

Bobby grabbed Jennifer's hand, even as he punched a preprogrammed number on the phone. He wasn't about to leave her on the ground where he couldn't protect her.

13

JENNIFER'S MIND WAS REELING as Bobby tugged her along with him and entered a huge warehouse where a small puddle jumper of a plane sat in wait. A man lingered by the wing, talking on his cell phone.

"We're going up, Chris," Rocky shouted, heading toward the passenger's entrance of the aircraft with Bobby and Jennifer in his wake. "Get ready to rev up that engine."

Chris shoved off the plane, ending his call. "What the—?"

"Do it!" Rocky shouted. "I need to be in the air in a flash, and beside the Bluejay." He eyed Bobby, Jennifer by his side. "That's the plane B.J. is in. It's a gamble, but with two planes in the air, B.J. makes the Bluejay the most likely to be the one with the bad chute." He eyed his watch. "They do twelve minutes of air maneuvers. We have roughly seven minutes to stop those jumpers, and that's if B.J. doesn't convince them to jump early."

Bobby gave a quick nod and asked Rocky several questions about B.J. and Gavin, before he yanked out a cell phone and dialed. Then, "I have a Charlie Fox-trot, I repeat, an effed-up situation getting worse. Two confirmed members of the cartel, both armed and dangerous, both ex-Special Forces, in active aggressive action with several hundred civilians on-site." He went on to explain Gavin's and B.J.'s positions and confirmed Rocky as cleared of suspicion.

Jennifer was gaping; Bobby knew about whatever it was that was going on here. He not only knew, he was on duty. He wasn't here for her, or for the wedding. He was here for his job.

He ended his call and gave Rocky a sharp nod. "We're set," he assured him.

Jennifer felt sick to her stomach and she turned toward the exit, ready to get away from Bobby. She was determined to go help Shari—somehow, someway— and then get the heck out of here, and out of Bobby's life, once and for all. She couldn't believe what a fool she'd been to believe Bobby had come back for her. Because deep down, as much as she hadn't been willing to admit it, that was what she'd thought, that was what she hoped.

"Go, Chris!" Rocky yelled. "Get us up beside the Bluejay, and do it now!"

Suddenly, Jennifer was lifted off the ground. She yelped in surprise, But there was no stopping the forward movement of her body; Bobby was behind her, his strong arms and body maneuvering her into the plane.

In protest, Jennifer whirled around to confront him, but the engine roared to life and swallowed her words before they were spoken. Bobby maneuvered her toward the wall and started to strap her with a parachute.

"Bobby, no!" she said, shouting to be heard. "I'm not jumping out of this plane."

He dropped to one knee in front of her, putting some sort of harness around her leg. "Good," he called out. "I don't want you to. But if for any reason, you have to, this chute will auto-deploy at the right altitude. I'll be nearby to make sure you're safe."

"If I'm being forced to jump out of a plane, Bobby, you failed to keep me safe!" She tried to get by him. "Let me off!" The plane started to move, and she fought to pass Bobby. He held her firmly, easily, as if no effort was exerted. "Let me off!"

He pulled her close, his lips near her ear. "I won't leave you on the ground where I can't look after you."

The plane was already moving, taxiing onto the runway, and there wasn't anything she could do but accept that she was going up when it did. "Let me go!" she repeated.

He eased back, holding her stare. Then he reached forward and tightened several straps to pull her chute into place. He leaned close. "If anything happens to the pilot, you jump. If you think something is going to happen to the plane, you jump. Understood?"

"Yes," she said. She understood all right—he'd come back and dragged her into hell all over again. Breaking her heart wasn't enough. He had to scare the crap out of her, as well.

She watched him strap on his own chute, mesmerized by the confident way he moved, by the primal readiness he wore as a second skin—in touch with that animal side we all possess. Ready to hunt, fight, survive. He wasn't going to let anyone die on his watch.

Suddenly, anger turned to pride. He was going to

save lives today. He *had* saved lives. Nothing else mattered. The plane jerked off the runway into the air, wind whistling around them.

Jennifer curled into the corner, as far from the door as possible. Bobby and Rocky were the opposite, fearlessly at the edge of the gaping hole that led to a steep drop down.

They pulled up next to another plane, and divers crowded at the plane's door. Rocky was shouting and cutting his hands through the air. Bobby, too. "No jump! No jump!"

Relief washed over Jennifer as the stunt divers seemed to understand. Hand signals were exchanged. The plane was going to land. But Jennifer looked out the window, and the divers from other planes were gone— they'd jumped. She hoped and prayed they were safe. At least, no one had jumped from the plane with B.J. inside—the one they knew had a bad parachute.

Jennifer gasped. Not a second after she had the thought, as she watched, someone jumped from B.J.'s plane. "B.J.!" Rocky shouted to Bobby and urgently motioned to the other divers. "No jump!" Then he turned to Bobby. "I'm going after him!" Rocky didn't wait for an answer. He jumped.

Jennifer's eyes went wide at his sudden departure, her gaze cutting to Bobby as he inched to the edge of the doorway. "I love you, Jennifer!" he yelled over the engine and wind. "I've always loved you." And just like that, Bobby was over the edge as well, leaving Jennifer in stunned disbelief.

Jennifer forgot fear for herself and charged forward, hanging on to the edge of the doorway and staring down at Bobby, who was shooting toward the earth, head-first, his body a tight, bulletlike shell.

Had he confessed love because he thought he wasn't going to make it through this jump? Her stomach rolled. "Please, Bobby, be okay," she whispered into the wind.

BOBBY CURSED the automatic chute when it opened, slowing down his progress. He could see B.J. and Rocky on the ground, fighting.

"Damn it!" he shouted and yanked a knife from his hip pocket. He cut his chute, picking up speed again. At the last possible moment, he pulled his backup chute, and came in hard to the right of where the other two men had landed.

He disconnected himself, more than ready to get a piece of B.J., but quickly pulled up as he realized B.J. was holding a gun on Rocky.

Everything went slow motion then. Rocky's gaze flickered to Bobby. B.J. began to turn. Bobby threw his knife, landing it in B.J.'s right shoulder, his right hand holding the pistol, dropping for an instant.

Rocky was on top of B.J. in a flash, rolling with B.J. in a desperate scramble that jarred the gun free. Bobby took the right moment to kick the gun away.

A chopper sounded in the distance. Help had arrived. Bobby grabbed the gun and aimed it at B.J., the noise rendering conversation impossible.

Once the bird was down, several armed soldiers rushed forward, led by Bobby's own team—the Crazy Aces—with Caleb in the lead. B.J. was cuffed and loaded for transport in a matter of minutes.

Back at the airfield a short while later, Bobby found

Caleb waiting for him in the hangar, and while he should have been surprised, he'd learned to expect the unexpected.

"What do we have going on here on the ground?" Bobby questioned immediately, Rocky nearby.

"Shari's safe," Caleb reported. "Gavin's in custody and the property is being cleared." He nodded at Rocky. "In conjunction with local law enforcement, the Army is shutting you down for investigation, effective immediately."

Rocky slid a rough hand over his jaw and turned away, staring out at the cluster of activity on the airfield, police and EMS vehicles lining the edges. The bleachers were quickly being emptied, hundreds of people scattering.

Bobby stepped closer to his side, noting Jennifer's plane on the ground in his peripheral vision. "I know you're innocent," Bobby said. "I'll speak on your behalf."

"Thanks, man," Rocky said. "But speaking on my behalf isn't going to undo the damage this is doing to my revenue stream. Don't get me wrong. I'm not ungrateful for what you guys did here tonight. Unfortunately, Gavin took the Hotzone to the sewer with him. Business was slim pickings in this economy anyway. These bimonthly shows helped me stay afloat. Who's going to want to come to another one after this?"

"You might be surprised," Bobby suggested. "People love to be in the middle of a scandal. It's like a rubbernecking holiday."

"I'm done," Rocky announced, clearly not amused by the joke. "I'm going to sell and get the hell out." He turned to Caleb. "Who needs me and for what? Let's get the information over with, and whatever else needs to be done. All of it."

Bobby understood Rocky wanting the inquisition over, though he doubted Rocky had any confessions to reveal. Bobby, on the other hand did—to Jennifer—and he'd made it on that plane. Or rather—he'd made his confession. He'd told Jennifer he still loved her. But he wasn't foolish enough to believe that got him out of hot water. Based on what she'd seen and heard tonight, she'd believe he had come back because of his duty. Words weren't enough. He had to prove to her he was back for her.

JENNIFER'S PLANE HAD BUMPED to a rough landing, the sky speckled with colorful skydivers and parachutes. B.J.'s plane—minus B.J.—had landed before theirs. Now, with engines dying to a hum, the doors opened, and a man in military fatigues poked his head in the doorway.

"Howdy there, ma'am," he said. "Name's Ryan Walker. You Jennifer?"

"Yes," she said anxiously, clinging to the wall for stability and quickly doing her best to wrestle off the parachute. "I'm Jennifer. Is Bobby okay?"

"Bobby's safe," he reported.

Her shoulders loosened with relief and the loss of the chute. "And everyone else?"

"Everyone else, too." He tilted a mike attached to his ear toward his mouth. "Tell Bobby she's wheels on the ground and safe, if he doesn't already know." Then to Jennifer. "I guess I see why he hasn't signed his reenlistment papers."

Her eyes went wide. "Bobby is up for reenlistment?"

Ryan frowned. "I guess I wasn't supposed to say that." He offered her his hand. "How about we get you out of here and negotiate your terms of silence?"

Her head swam, her thoughts a jumbled mess. Bobby was up for reenlistment and hadn't told her.

"What the hell, Ryan," Bobby called out from the side of the plane, out of her visual. "You couldn't be without me for a couple of weeks or what?"

Ryan turned to where Bobby was; although he remained out of Jennifer's range of sight still, she could hear the two men exchange a few words about B.J. Jennifer moved to the edge of the plane's doorway, planning to jump down, but it was too steep. So she stood there, fuming, telling herself this was not the time to talk to Bobby about his reenlistment, or rather, his failure to tell her about it.

He'd let Marcie believe he was here for her wedding. But he was here for duty. He was here for a job. Not for her... No, she thought, her heart squeezing. Not for her.

Her heart pounded in her ears even as thunder rumbled in the night air, the moon barely visible, the airfield lights blasting a hole in the darkness to illuminate the skydivers. A flash of lightning shot through the black circle around them, one of those sudden, Texas summer thunderstorms, ready to rip and roar. How appropriate, because right now, Jennifer was ready to blow up a storm of her own.

Ryan continued to egg Bobby on with a playful jest that spoke of friendship and of a part of Bobby's life as foreign to her as the man who'd jumped out of that plane.

"I love an excuse to come to my sweetheart home state," Ryan said. "Besides, you know you can't live without me."

"Don't count on that one," Bobby said dryly, rounding the corner of the plane, with Ryan by his side, and bringing Jennifer into focus.

Her heart froze. She couldn't hold back. She didn't care who was watching, or who was listening. This explosion was years in the making. It needed to erupt. "You came here to do a job," she blurted out. "Not for the wedding. Not for me, which is fine, Bobby. Fine. But don't tell me you love me. Don't play these stupid games with me. Maybe they work for you. But they don't work for me. They hurt. I don't even know who you are that you would want to hurt me."

Shadowy turbulence flitted across his face. "I would never hurt you—"

"You left me without a word for seven years," she hissed. "Yes. Yes, you would hurt me."

"I was trying to protect you," he said, "because I love you."

She drew her spine stiff. "Is that why you didn't tell me you were up for reenlistment? You wanted to keep your options open, and you thought telling me that would hurt me?"

"Ah, sorry, Bobby," Ryan said. "And they want us in the office."

"I didn't tell you because I didn't want you to feel any pressure," he said.

She hardly knew what to say to that. "There is no pressure," she said. "You left. I don't want you back."

She walked to the other side of the doorway where Ryan had discreetly stepped. "Please help me down, Sergeant Walker."

Bobby made a frustrated sound and was in front of her, grabbing hold of her hips in an instant. Before she could stop him, he'd slid her down the front of his body, molding her close, her feet dangling off the ground. He was warm and hard, and she wanted to hit him and kiss him at the same time.

"We'll talk when this is over," he vowed.

"You and Ryan can talk," she said. "About your life. The one I'm not a part of."

"Jennifer—"

She shoved on his shoulders. "Put me down, Bobby."

"This isn't over, Jennifer."

"So you keep saying," she said. "But you see…it is over. It was over seven years ago. I am just finally willing to admit that."

BOBBY WASN'T ABOUT to take that answer from Jennifer. Not now. Not ever again. He set her on the ground, snagged her hand and cut Ryan a hard look. "She was never here."

"Understood," Ryan said.

"Make sure everyone else, Rocky included, understands," Bobby ordered, and was already walking, pulling Jennifer along with him. "I don't want you anywhere near these people Rocky is involved with."

"Then you shouldn't have brought me here and pretended it was a date," she said.

"I'm glad we agree it was a date," he said, casting her a sideways look. "Because it was."

"A date is not a mission to take down some drug lord, Bobby," she said. "You used me as an excuse to come here."

"Bringing you here was a mistake," he said. "I know that. It's dangerous. Exactly why— Now isn't the time for this conversation."

She grabbed his hand. "Bobby, wait."

He stopped walking and slid his fingers to her face. Raindrops began to pelt down on top of them; the cold splattering, a contrast to the hot summer night. "I need you to walk fast and get out of here before someone decides you should be a witness, and you become a target for some very nasty people. Understand?"

She visibly paled and nodded. He took her hand and made a quick path between the buildings, to the parking lot. Cars were lined up, exiting the graveled path. The rain pounded into the rocks and dirt, and clung to their clothes, wetting their skin.

Bobby stopped at the driver's side of the rental and pulled Jennifer into his arms, his mouth slanting over hers in a passionate kiss that defied the cold rain pounding down around them. He drank of her with wild abandon, blocked out the weather, blocked out his duty. Afraid this would be the last taste of her, the last, sweet, blissful piece of Jennifer he ever had, and telling her without words how much she meant to him. And she kissed him back, clinging to him, wildly taking from him, giving to him, as if she, too, feared this was the end.

It took every piece of willpower he possessed to pull back, his hands framing the damp strands of hair dripping around her heart-shaped face. "I was already here when I was called to duty. I'll explain everything later, but you have to go now. Jennifer...I do love you." He kissed her forehead. "Go now."

He started to back away, and she held on to his arm. "I..."

She was afraid to say it, afraid of getting hurt. He offered her an escape. "You have to go." He opened the car door and motioned her inside. She hesitated a moment and climbed in.

The minute the engine roared to life, Bobby took off running. And this time he vowed, he wasn't running from Jennifer, or from himself. He was going to run to her. That was, if she would still have him.

After tonight, he knew she wanted him. He knew she probably even loved him. He just wasn't sure she believed love was enough.

14

BOBBY WAS UP FOR reenlistment and he hadn't told her. The implications of those two pieces of information shaped the horrible, rain-drenched drive, filled with inner turmoil and confusion, far more than his confession of love.

Jennifer had always believed he'd loved her on some level, even after he left. But did he love her enough? His silence about his reenlistment seemed to confirm the answer as no. Even if his duty had come after his arrival, his silence said he still wasn't committed enough to her, to them as a couple. And that was hard to swallow. Nevertheless, she was ready to swallow it. Ready to be done with this. No more flings. No more games.

She pulled up to her condo, the interior of the car a sopping wet mess from her clothes, and rushed to the door, the rain still coming down so hard she officially understood the saying "it was raining barrels." She unlocked the door, to be greeted by a meowing kitty. She offered a few kitty pets and a little kitty talk, then stripped, eager for a hot shower.

An hour later, near ten already, hair dry, her face

scrubbed fresh, Jennifer sat on her couch, the air cranked on high, and snuggled beneath a white down comforter. She had a cup of hot chocolate in her hand despite the season; it was like her comfort food in a mug—warm and sweet. Maybe because it reminded her of family and holidays.

Beneath the blanket, she wore pink sweatpants and a pink tank top, a bra most defiantly in place in her determination to be casually pulled together with a strong, not sexy, appeal. Okay, so maybe pink wasn't the best way to send the strong message, but she'd changed three times and this was the best she could come up with.

Sipping her chocolate, with Julie curled in a ball at her feet, she told herself to stay angry at Bobby, to end any relationship with him tonight. Maybe if she drank enough chocolate bliss, she wouldn't need any Bobby bliss. She sighed at the fallibility of that strategy. She fiddled with the remote, but didn't turn on the television.

Instead, she sat there, processing, thinking. And the longer she sat on that couch, the more she saw beyond her own emotions. Bobby had been brave tonight, honorable. She didn't know the Bobby who jumped out of planes and saved lives. Or did she? He'd been a strong, steady, dependable friend during the party when the guests had gotten out of control. Maybe he was born to be a soldier. Pride welled inside her.

"He's trying to choose between me and the Army," she whispered. Her hand went to her stomach, feeling suddenly queasy. He didn't want her to know about the reenlistment in case he chose the Army. And how could she ask him to choose her? She'd seen him today— seen how he'd acted to save lives. How could anything compare? Maybe this wasn't a fling. Maybe it was simply two people in love whose destinies couldn't be one. Maybe rather than giving him ultimatums, she simply needed to love him while she could. To love him enough to tell him it was okay that he be who he was, that he be the soldier he'd become.

Reaching for the remote again, Jennifer hoped for something to occupy her mind, rather than sit there and think herself into some sort of insanity. At the same moment, a knock sounded on the door. She jumped and the remote went flying, her heart exploding in her chest. Julie screeched and jumped. Jennifer pressed her hand to her face. Good grief, so much for seeming together.

Jennifer threw back the blanket and rushed to the door. "Hello?"

"It's Bobby," he said, his voice a familiar rough sandpaper that both stroked her nerves and aroused her senses.

Jennifer opened the door to find him standing there, his clothes wet, his blond hair lying haphazardly framing his strong features, a swatch across his brow. The rain splattered around him, jumping off the awning that wasn't enough to protect him from being any more beaten and weathered. And he did indeed look weathered and worn, tired from no sleep the night before, the expression on his face stark, as if he expected her to turn him away.

"I should never have taken you there tonight," he admitted. "I was called to investigate the Hotzone, and I selfishly didn't want to give up time with you. I put you in danger."

Her heart squeezed, the need to reach for him too

great to ignore. She stepped forward and forgot the rain, flinging her arms around him and holding him tight.

"You were a real-life hero tonight, Bobby," she said, pressing her head to his chest, his heart racing against her ear. "I was proud of you." His shirt was wet, but the warmth of his skin seeped through into hers. The strength of his arms closed around her.

"Jennifer," he whispered, lifting her and setting her back down inside the house, kicking the door shut. "Sweetheart—"

"I don't care about how, or why, we went to that show tonight," she said, tilting her head up to stare at him. "I don't even care why you came into town."

"I swear to you, Jennifer," he said, framing her face. "I was assigned the task after I arrived. I came for the wedding." His voice softened. "I came for you."

She wet her lips, her mouth and throat dry. "I believe you," she promised. "But, Bobby…tonight I saw the soldier in you. It's in your blood. I'm not asking you to walk away from that for me, and I know that's what you think you have to do. But you don't. You can't. You have to be who, and what, you are."

He blinked down at her, shadows flickering in the depths of his eyes, his voice whisky-rough. "*You're* in my blood, Jennifer." His mouth came down on hers, firm, strong like the man, his tongue sliding past her lips, demanding, claiming. Wild. They were wild. She was on her toes, or maybe he was lifting her. She didn't know, didn't care. This was the first time since his arrival that she let herself completely enjoy Bobby. Completely accepting that what they had been didn't matter nearly as much as what they were here and now.

Her hands found the hem of his shirt, shoving the damp cotton upward. "Take it off," she ordered.

Bobby yanked it over his head, tossing it on the floor, giving her a delicious eyeful of muscle. Her hands traced the hot flesh, and she cast him a tiny, seductive smile. "I love your soldier tough-guy abs of yours."

"Oh, yeah?" His voice held a smile, rather than the duress, the torment, of minutes before.

"Hmm," she concurred, her smile fading when her gaze lifted and latched on to his, the sizzle between them so much deeper than simple attraction. Heat shimmered along her nerve endings, desire pooling deep in her belly.

He picked her up, palms intimately wrapping around her backside. Her hips cradled his, his erection thick, pulsing against her. "I want you to like my body, Jennifer," he said, his voice low, taut; he nipped her neck. "I need a shower." He nipped her neck again, then her lips. "Care to join me?"

She curled her fingers together behind his neck. "It's my shower," she teased. "I most definitely get to join the hot, naked soldier in it."

He kissed her then, a fevered frenzy coming over them, and she wasn't sure they would make it to the shower anytime soon. All that mattered was touching, tasting, feeling.

Until a sudden pounding sounded at the door, jerking their mouths apart. Bobby murmured, "What the—?"

"Jennifer! It's Marcie. Let me in. It's raining!"

Jennifer's eyes went wide, her hands resting on Bobby's shoulders. "It's close to midnight. Something must be wrong."

Bobby set Jennifer down, snagging his shirt and

pulling it over his head even as Jennifer jerked the door open.

The rain was coming down in buckets again, and Marcie rushed in the door, dripping wet. "Mark and I broke up," she sobbed. "The wedding is off!"

"What?!" Jennifer exclaimed.

"The wedding isn't off, Marcie," Bobby said calmly. "You're just upset."

Marcie nodded. "It's off. He hates me. We hate each other." A panicked look flashed across her face as she focused on Bobby. "Uh, I didn't know you were here. I should have known you'd be here." She burst into tears, her teeth chattering. "Don't worry. I'm leaving." She turned to the door.

"No!" Jennifer and Bobby said at the same time. Bobby quickly pressed his hand to the door. "Stay. I'll go talk to Mark."

Marcie whirled around. "It won't do any good. He hates me, Bobby. He hates me."

"He doesn't hate you," Bobby assured her.

"He does," she said, mascara running down her cheeks. "And I'm dripping all over your floor."

Jennifer knew a hot-bath, glass-of-wine crisis when she saw one. "I'll get a towel," she said and started to turn away before adding, "And you and Mark are going to make up, Marcie. You watch and see."

"We won't," Marcie insisted. "You don't know how bad it is."

Jennifer had a good idea. She'd seen them fighting. But she didn't comment, not about to make matters worse.

"You've been trying to push him away, Marcie,"

Bobby said as Jennifer walked toward the hall closet, silently agreeing with his assessment.

Jennifer started a hot bath with bubbles and then rushed back to Marcie with a big, fluffy towel in hand but stopped at the edge of the hallway as she heard what Marcie was saying.

"And you're any better, Bobby?" Marcie demanded. "You ran away so Jennifer wouldn't push you away when you became like your father. Well…I can't have kids. Mark can never be a father if he marries me. I thought I could deal with that, but he's going to resent me down the road."

"So that's it?" Bobby challenged. "You're trying to make him hate you now, because you think he'll hate you later?"

"No," she said. "No, I… He says it doesn't matter. But what's he supposed to say?"

"He'd find a reason to walk away if he wanted to walk away," Bobby replied.

Jennifer felt as if she'd been slugged in the chest. Bobby had found his reason to leave.

"Do you love him?" Bobby asked.

"Yes," Marcie said. "I love him."

"Then why can't you just let him love you?"

She started bawling again. "Because I'm scared, Bobby."

Jennifer had heard enough and rounded the corner, expecting to go to Marcie's rescue. Instead, she found Bobby pulling a dripping-wet Marcie into his arms and hugging her, a big brother taking care of his little sister. Bobby looked up and his gaze captured Jennifer's. "Then do what I didn't," he said. "Tell him you're scared. Let him help you."

Jennifer sucked in a shaky breath, feeling his words clear to her soul. He was talking to her. He was telling her he'd been scared. Telling her he was still scared.

"I don't know how," Marcie said, grabbing Bobby's arms and pleading. "Will you talk to him? He's so mad. I don't know what to say, and I know you don't know him well, but—"

"I'll talk to him."

"Now?" she asked hopefully.

"Yes," he said. "Now."

Jennifer stepped forward and wrapped Marcie in the towel. "To the bathroom and get in that hot tub. I even put some of that calming eucalyptus in the water you gave me on my birthday. I'll bring you wine and we'll talk."

Marcie nodded and headed to the bath.

Bobby made sure he had Jennifer's cell programmed properly into his phone. They stood toe to toe, the silent, unspoken words wrapping them with a mixture of hot sun and cold winter snow, too complex and textured to touch on now.

"Thank you for doing this," Jennifer said. "I know you haven't slept."

"I'm not worried about sleep," he said. "I'm worried about Marcie and Mark working this out before their wedding."

"Yes," she said, her hand resting on his chest. There was so much she wanted to say. "You'll come back?"

He scooped her into his arms and kissed her. "I'm not going anywhere this time, Jennifer." His lips brushed hers and then he was gone.

Jennifer stood there, stunned. Confused. He was leaving. He was staying. He was up for reenlistment, but obviously, clearly after today, a soldier. He wore the title well, wore it with honor.

Jennifer's cell phone started ringing, startling her into action. She rushed forward, to the table where she'd set her purse. Marcie appeared in the hallway, still fully dressed, a hopeful look on her face that had Jennifer saying, "It's probably Mark, worried about you."

"Don't answer it if it is," she said. "He doesn't want to marry me, he doesn't deserve to know where I'm at."

Jennifer blinked in confusion. "You just asked Bobby to go talk to him."

"I know, but…" Marcie pressed her palm to her forehead. "I don't know anymore."

Jennifer grabbed her purse on the hall table and checked caller ID on her phone. "It's him," she said.

"He doesn't want to marry me, Jen," Marcie said, mascara dropping down her cheeks.

"He wants to marry you," Jennifer said. "This is just cold feet before the wedding." The phone stopped ringing.

"See!" Marcie said. "He already gave up."

"It's Saturday night," Jennifer said. "And mark my words, by next Sunday night, you will be a married woman enjoying the first day of her honeymoon." The phone started ringing again and she answered it.

"Is she there?" Mark asked, his voice steely hard.

"Yes."

"That's all I wanted to know," he said and hung up.

Jennifer pulled the phone from her ear, stunned by Mark's abruptness.

"He didn't even ask to speak to me?" Marcie asked, her face already crinkling.

"You didn't want to talk to him," Jennifer said, trying to talk her way out of this. Marcie burst into tears.

It was a good while later when Jennifer managed to bundle Marcie up in silk pajamas. They sat on the bed and talked.

"Everything was perfect until we decided to get married," she said. "Now it's a mess." She sipped her wine and set it on the nightstand. "If I need to stay here until I find a place, you won't mind, right?"

"You won't need a place to stay," Jennifer told her, "but, of course." She took Marcie's hand. "It's going to work out."

Marcie studied her. "It didn't for you and Bobby," she said. "And you wanted it to. You still do. But it won't happen. You know why? The same reason Bobby and I are friends. Because we both have enough baggage to sink a warship. We aren't the forever kind of people. You and Mark picked wrong. There is no happy ending."

Jennifer had a moment of clarity. She'd spent seven years looking for an ending. Bobby had run from an ending. Marcie was running from an ending. She reached out and took Marcie's hand. "Love doesn't have an ending," Jennifer said. "We both need to stop trying to find one."

She loved Bobby. She would always love Bobby. Closure didn't mean she stopped loving him. In fact, it meant she'd stopped denying she loved him. It meant she had to figure out what kind of spot that love filled in her life.

THE RAIN HAD, AT LEAST, temporarily stopped, the moon peeking through a tunnel of clouds, but not a star could be seen. Nor was there a light to be found

in Mark and Marcie's house when Bobby pulled into
the driveway and parked behind Mark's truck. It was
a bad sign. Bobby ground his teeth and climbed out of
the car. Either Mark was gone, probably drinking off
his troubles with the guys—trouble waiting to happen.
Or Mark was in bed asleep, unaffected by his fight with
Marcie—bigger trouble. As in the kind that meant the
wedding was really off.

Bobby started up the stairs when Mark leaned forward in a deck chair, the moon illuminating shadowy
features. "I see she sent in reinforcements," Mark said.
"Save your breath. I'm done. Marrying me is supposed
to be making Marcie happy. I've never seen her so
miserable. And don't tell me it's nerves. It's more than
that."

Bobby sat down on the steps, not worried about
the wet concrete, considering he had been dried and
drenched several times over that day. "She thinks you
hate her. She thinks you don't want to marry her."

"I love her, man," he said. "I love her so much it
hurts. But she can't have babies, and she thinks that is
somehow going to destroy my life. I told her we'd get a
dog. Heck, if that doesn't satisfy the paternal instinct,
we'll get a cat, too. We'll flipping adopt, if necessary.
But she can't get over this. Or maybe she doesn't want to
get over it. I pressured her into setting a date, into putting the baby thing aside. Well, no more pressure. Like
I said. I'm done. I get that I'm not important enough to
her to get by this thing. That I'm not 'the guy' or we'd
fight this battle together. I have to let her go so she can
find the person who is 'the guy.' I love her enough to
know I have to let her go so she can find that person."

No more pressure. That was what Jennifer had said

to him. Mark believed Marcie didn't love him enough to overcome her fears. Mark planned to let Marcie go. Just as Jennifer planned to let him go, unless Bobby convinced her otherwise.

15

IT WAS THREE in the morning now, officially, and Jennifer was so darn glad her clinic was closed for the day. She and Marcie had been sitting at Jennifer's glossy mahogany kitchen table, talking, for hours, coffee mugs and their second bag of chocolate kisses—Jennifer had snuck them for herself from the party supplies—sitting between them.

"I'm convinced," Jennifer moaned, shoving her cup away, "whoever said chocolate cures all didn't eat a bag and a half of kisses and drink three cups of hot chocolate. Thankfully, we put our loose-fitting sweats on. I need breathing room."

"Wimp," Marcie said, unwrapping another candy.

"What happened to herbal tea and granola?" Jennifer asked.

"They help maintain a healthy life," Marcie said, holding up her now bare-naked, ready-to-eat, chocolate kiss. "But chocolate heals the soul and the soul is the window to everything else." She popped the candy into her mouth.

"Unless you get sick first," Jennifer said. "Which

apparently would be appropriate in my case because my soul doesn't feel one bit healed and my stomach is pretty angry about the situation."

Marcie pushed the candy bag in Jennifer's direction. "I was sick ten kisses ago. Eat more. It gets better."

"No, thank you," Jennifer said emphatically. "No more for me."

Marcie stared at her, the somber look slipping back across her features. "You should call Bobby," Marcie suggested. "He's been gone a long time."

"Let them have their guy time, Marcie," she urged gently as she had several times already.

"What if Bobby hasn't even found Mark?" Marcie said. "Maybe he's looking for him and doesn't want me to know. What if Mark is off at some bar hanging all over some new woman? What if—"

"Marcie," Jennifer interrupted. "Don't. Stop. You're making yourself crazy. Imagining things that just aren't so. Mark loves you."

"Yeah, well, you and Bobby are living proof sometimes love isn't enough."

Jennifer flinched as if slapped. "That was low."

"Oh, no," Marcie said. "I'm sorry. I didn't mean to be thoughtless. I didn't mean it as an insult at all. Just the opposite. I know how much you and Bobby love each other and still you've been apart the past seven years. Love doesn't necessarily remove all obstacles. I know you know that. Love isn't the easy answer."

Jennifer grabbed a chocolate. Suddenly, her stomach didn't hurt as much as her soul needed healing. "Maybe you should just have sex with Mark," she suggested dryly. "Isn't that what you suggested I do with Bobby?"

"I do have sex with Mark," she assured Jennifer. "You weren't having sex with Bobby. There's a difference." She picked up Julie and hugged her. "I love this cat. She is so sweet."

Jennifer might have agreed but the chocolate hit her stomach hard. "Okay, for the record. Sex hasn't solved anything. Chocolate makes me sick. Love isn't always enough. I'm not sure where that leaves either of us. I don't know what to do, Marcie."

A knock sounded on the door. "You get it!" Marcie whispered, scrambling wildly to fix her hair and straighten in her chair. "That's what you do." She waved Jennifer on. "Hurry!"

"I'm trying," Jennifer said, unfolding her legs from where she'd tucked them beneath her and rushing to the door about the time she heard, "Jen, it's Bobby."

She yanked the door open, to find him clean-shaven and showered, the spicy scent uniquely him, making her wonder how she ever thought chocolate held a candle to sex—at least, sex with Bobby. The rain had stopped and he was dry, but his eyes were weary, heavy-lidded. Even the macho hot soldier couldn't hide his exhaustion.

"Come in," she urged for the second time in a night.

He took a step forward and passed her and, to Jennifer's surprise, Mark followed. "Mark!" Marcie yelled and charged forward into his arms, all but knocking Jennifer and Bobby into the wall.

Mark kissed Marcie, long and hard, and then they disappeared into the bedroom. Jennifer's bedroom. "That went better than expected," Bobby said, chuckling as he pulled her off the wall where she'd leaned to avoid collision. He directed her toward the living room.

"At least until the chocolate and sex wears off," Jennifer said skeptically.

Bobby sat down on the couch and took her with him. "Why did you say that like chocolate and sex were bad things? I think we've proven otherwise." He tugged off his boots.

"The chocolate and sex are great," she agreed. "But when they're done, when it's over—then what?"

"They'll figure it out," he said, and then pulled Jennifer and the blanket down on top of him as he lay on his back, head on the pillow cushion. "Just like we will."

He molded her close and she settled against him. The effect was warm and intimate. "Until you leave again."

"Why would I leave, Jen?" he asked softly. "I finally came home."

She lifted her head at that, opening her mouth to ask what that meant but his eyes were shut, his lips hinting at a satisfied smile. Slowly, she slid back down, resting her head on his chest, letting his heartbeat thrum beneath her palm. His strong shoulder cradled her head. Her lashes lowered, and she, too, felt the hint of a smile on her lips as she drifted off to sleep.

BOBBY WOKE TO THE SOUND OF whispers, male and female. He blinked awake, sunlight piercing a line through the curtains, the clock reading nine o'clock. Awareness rushed through him as he felt the sweet warmth of Jennifer resting in his arms, a smile touching his lips as he realized her cat, Julie, was on top of his legs. They'd left Mark and Marcie in the bedroom to talk things out and fallen asleep on the couch. This was a little slice of heaven. This was how he wanted to wake up every day of his life for the rest of his life. He wasn't sure what that meant—he only knew that this was why'd held off on reenlistment. He needed more than duty in his life.

Jennifer lifted her head and turned to look over the edge of the couch. Marcie and Mark were tiptoeing toward the door. "Does this mean I still have to wear the lime dress?" Jennifer asked.

Marcie huffed, no longer whispering, "It's yellow—"

"Green," Jennifer finished. "I know. Which isn't a real color by the way—but are you two happy now and I get to wear the yellow-green dress?"

"Yes," Mark said, wrapping his arms around Marcie from behind. "You are most definitely wearing the dress. And if you'll excuse us, I'm taking my soon-to-be wife home. Oh, and no skydiving for me. You two are on your own today."

Marcie smiled and turned to Mark, planting a kiss on him before they left. The door shut and Jennifer settled down on the couch, resting on one elbow, her hand on Bobby's cheek. "Whatever you said to Mark seemed to work. I just hope the baby thing doesn't become an issue in the future."

Julie stretched and walked over the top of Bobby before plopping down on his stomach.

Jennifer laughed and picked her up, cuddling her and then setting her on the ground. "She likes you."

"I like her, too," he said, reaching down and stroking Julie's back a moment before leaving the cat to its own entertainment as an idea came to him. He slid his hand behind his head and propped it up. "I know how to solve the baby problem for Marcie and Mark."

Jennifer's brows dipped. "How in the world would we do that?"

"We'll get them a Julie."

She laughed. "You want to get Mark and Marcie a cat?"

"Or a pet," he agreed. "Whatever kind you think will make them happy."

"Well," Jennifer said thoughtfully, "Marcie does love Julie and Oriental cats are very loving. They tend to become the babies of the house."

"So a 'Julie' would be perfect," he said. "We'll go get one today."

"It's not that easy," she said. "You don't just go get an Oriental shorthair. There's likely a waiting list and down payments on new litters."

"You're a vet," he said. "Surely you can pull strings."

She sighed. "I don't know. I could make some calls, but we might have to drive several hours."

"I'm willing if you're willing," he said.

She studied him. "I can't believe we're going to do this."

He smiled and rolled Jennifer beneath him. She was small and soft, and warm in all the right places. He was hot in all the right places, too. "You know what I think?"

She wrapped her fingers together behind his neck. "I'm almost afraid to ask."

"I think," he said, "we should make love, then go to Waffle House like we used to every Sunday morning and eat until we are miserable happily overstuffed. After that, we'll go in search of an Oriental shorthair."

"You do realize," she said slowly after a brief pause,

"what you suggest completely breaks the 'only sex' rule I set."

"I dare you to break the rule," he said, his lips lowering, lingering above hers. "Say you'll have more than sex with me for the day."

She laughed. "You're crazy."

"For you," he promised and kissed her. It was long minutes later when he sat on the couch, Jennifer on top of him, gloriously naked, the wet heat of her body wrapped around the hard length of him. Her breasts were high and full, her nipples rosy-pink pebbles pressed against his palms, taut against his tongue. Her kiss even sweeter than the addictive honey flavor he'd never get enough of, because he could taste the change in her, he could taste the unbridled passion—and he knew the walls were coming down. But as he spilled himself inside her, felt her spasm around him, cling to him, hold him, he knew she hadn't given herself fully to him, nor would she until she knew he'd done so to her. She deserved nothing less and he was trying desperately to find his way there.

For long seconds, they sat together, bodies merged intimately, foreheads together until Bobby noticed the cat was sitting on the arm of the couch watching them. "Okay, now," he said. "This is like some sort of weird voyeurism. We have to train the cat not to watch."

Jennifer laughed and kissed him. "I'll tell her to turn her back next time. Now. Take me to breakfast." Bobby stood up, still inside her. "I'll take you in the shower first. Waffle House does breakfast all day."

JENNIFER SAT IN THE Waffle House booth across from Bobby and finished up a returned call from a breeder. She hung up, feeling excited. "Finally," she declared. "We have success. They have an adult ready to retire—"

"Retire," Bobby said, stabbing a link of sausage. "Isn't a retired cat setting Marcie and Mark up for heartbreak?"

"Retired from being a show cat," she said. "She's only two. She's a great age. None of the kitten craziness. She's trained. Sweet and loving. Her name is Ella and she's at the opposite side of San Antonio. A couple of hours' drive."

"Ella it is then," he said. "You catch me up on the past seven years during the drive."

"You want another?" the cook asked, a fifty-something man who Jennifer suspected owned the Waffle House franchise.

Bobby patted his stomach. "I'm done in today," he said and glanced at Jennifer. "But we'll be back." Not phrased as "he'd be back" but *we*. His gaze held Jennifer's and she almost shivered with the warmth there, telling her he was going to spend every minute with her that he could.

"You better," the cook-maybe-owner said. "I like a couple with a healthy appetite."

Jennifer laughed as the man departed with Bobby's plate. "I bet he does. You ate three waffles, bacon, eggs and sausage. I've never seen you eat more than two waffles. You've expanded your horizons."

"Technically, it's breakfast and lunch," he said. "We never made it out of the house on Sundays before two." And they hadn't today either. He eyed his watch. "Right on time." He leaned forward, lowered his voice. "Just like old times."

"Indeed," she said softly, nostalgia a bittersweet thing this day but she wasn't fighting it. She was with Bobby, enjoying their limited time together. "No wonder I never eat a waffle without thinking of you."

He smiled and paid their check. "Funny," he said playfully, standing up and offering her his hand. "I've never had a waffle without thinking of you either."

She laughed and grabbed her purse, before slipping her fingers between his. "Glad to know a waffle reminds you of me."

They strolled across the parking lot, hand in hand, until they reached the passenger side of the car, a weeping willow grazing the roof and offering privacy and shade.

Bobby leaned against the car and molded Jennifer close. "Far more reminds me of you than I think you realize," he said. "I missed you. I missed us. I swear to you I never meant to hurt you. I love you. I never stopped loving you."

"The hardest part was not how you left," she admitted. "It was the seven years of silence." Her gaze lifted and she didn't try to hide the hurt. "I'd see something, or do something, that reminded me of you and that silence made me feel you never had those moments about me. You never called. You never wrote. For seven years, Bobby."

"I convinced myself you were better off without me," he said, his voice heavy, thick. "I pushed myself to the point of mental and physical exhaustion so I didn't have to think about anything but being a soldier. Fighting. Serving my country. I entered a special unit. I was never in the same place more than a few nights at once. And I saw it destroy the few men who tried to have relationships. How could I ask you to endure that life? But I'm up for reenlistment, Jen, and I don't have to go back." He laced his fingers around her neck. "I love you, Jennifer. I don't know if I can be the man you need. I don't know if you even will allow me to try. But I want to be."

The longing in his voice, the hope glistening in his eyes, washed over her. All the sorrow faded, became nothing more than a leaf fluttering in the shadow of a tree with years of history. "I love you, too," she confessed, her voice a rasp of a whisper. "But leaving the Army is a big step. You did so much good last night. You are amazing at what you do. Don't give that up for me. I've loved you since I met you. I can love you between missions."

"Getting out of the Army is purely selfish," he said. "In between missions isn't enough for me. I've had seven years of living out of a duffel bag, watching people die, trying to keep it from happening. I have enough nightmares to last me a lifetime. I'm ready to get out before they take over."

"What will you do?" she asked.

"I have an idea or two floating around in my head." He wiggled an eyebrow. "Women like firemen. Maybe I'll be a fireman. I bet we can have fun with a few 'hot' fantasies."

Jennifer laughed. "We can do that without you actually working for the fire department though."

"Ah, yes," he agreed, kissing her neck and then whispering in her ear. "We might have to go the fireman route tonight." His breath tickled her neck and sent a shiver down her spine.

"I'm not over the hot soldier fantasy yet," she said.

He leaned back. "One hot solider coming up," he said. "After we go pick up a cat named Ella. We should hurry." He lowered his lips near hers. "Maybe we'll get married and get Julie a sister."

She sucked in a breath. "Bobby."

He smiled against her lips. "I like it when you say my name." And he kissed her. Jennifer wrapped her arms around him, but even as she sank into the reassuring feel of his arms around her and holding her close, she knew there was still a barrier between them. A wall that could only come down when she knew nothing, and no one, could push his buttons and make him run again.

"Since we're all about the past being put to rest, and a bright shiny future," she said. "Why don't we get the meeting with your father out of the way? Ella is only about twenty minutes from his place."

Instant tension crackled off him but he was too smooth to even move an eyebrow. "No need to ruin a great day," he said and gave her a quick kiss, setting her away from him to open his door. "I've decided visiting my father is like giving him control he doesn't deserve." He winked. "Giving you control is much more fun."

16

BOBBY SETTLED INTO THE driver's seat, all too aware of Jennifer's piercing stare as he started the engine. He wanted a future with Jennifer. He damn sure wasn't letting his father mess it up. He was crazy to have ever considered going to see that man.

"Bobby," she said, a reprimand threading the one word.

"What?" he asked innocently, as if he didn't know she was still talking about his father. "I do like giving you control." He put the car in gear. "You're very sexy when you're feeling empowered."

"You know very well I'm talking about your father," she said, glaring at him.

"You, I give control to. Him—he gets none." He pulled the rental to the edge of the driveway. "Straight shot up I-35 to San Antonio, right?"

"Right," she said. "And don't change the subject."

"Since when is asking directions changing the subject?" he asked, enjoying the combative response, and the cute way her voice lifted when she was mad, despite his father being the source of her frustration. He regretted ever suggesting they go see him.

"You know very well San Antonio is a straight shot up the highway," she said. "What other way is there?"

Bobby opened his mouth to remind her he'd been gone seven years and she held up a hand. "I don't want an answer. Not to that question. To this one. You said you wanted to see your father. You need to see your father. It's been a long time."

He gave her a quick glance and maneuvered onto the highway. "I'm still waiting for the question. Because I didn't hear one in there anywhere."

She crossed her arms. "There's no question, after all. Because I'm not asking. We're going to see your father."

"A waste of time when we could be enjoying each other," he said. He'd given this a lot of thought. He was glad he'd been detoured from seeing his father. He wasn't giving his father a chance to mess up what he had going with Jennifer again.

"You said—" she began.

"I know what I said," he agreed. "I thought visiting him proved he had no control over me. But I was wrong. It gives him control. As if he decides my future, or worse, our future. He doesn't. The whole point is that he never had any control over me, he never decided who I was, or what I would become. It was my youthful perception and immaturity." He glanced over at her, settling the car into cruise control. "He doesn't matter. We do."

She reached out and took his hand. Hers was soft and delicate and perfect against his. He wanted to hold it forever; he wanted to be here with her.

"Please, Bobby," she said. "Get this behind you. You need to face this." She hesitated a second. "And if your father drove you away from me, I need to know he can't do it again."

He cut her a fast sideways look. "He can't. He won't." An acidy burn rasped through his throat and then exploded in his chest. "And I don't want to ruin our day together."

"We can purchase Ella today, but pick her up after the honeymoon," she suggested. "That's better, anyway. Then we can go see your father on the way back."

"A destructive ending to a perfect day," he said dryly. "No, thank you."

"It ends with you and me, not him," she reminded him. "And he does have power over you if he can ruin our day. He has power over us. Let's take that from him."

"I don't need to prove anything to him, Jennifer," he said. "I don't want to try anymore."

"You were determined to see him yesterday. What changed today?"

"I thought I had to see him to prove something to you and me," he explained. "But that's exactly what I've done for seven years—prove I'm not like him. I'm done with that. No more."

"He's your father," she insisted. "You haven't seen him in seven years. When was the last time you actually talked to him?"

"A year ago," he said. "He cussed me out, slurring every other word because I sent him five hundred dollars instead of the six hundred he asked me for. I was overseas, and it was all I could do from there."

She inhaled softly and drew her hand from his. He

felt a razor-sharp jab in his chest. She'd decided this defined their relationship in some way and fool that he was, he'd put that idea in her head.

"Let's go buy Ella," he said. "We'll see how late it is when we're heading back."

She cast him a smile that shined as brightly as a Christmas tree. "I'm so glad you're going to do this."

He grimaced. "I said we'd see how late it is."

Her eyes twinkled. "I know."

Which meant she had every intention of forcing him to see his father. "You're stubborn as a rock when you want something."

"I prefer persuasive," she said, reaching over and sliding her fingers between his again. "For instance, after we see your father, I was thinking about a few hot soldier fantasies." She drew his hand to her mouth and kissed it, casting him a seductive look that shot straight to his groin.

"I didn't say we were going to see my father," he reminded her, glancing between her and the road. "I said we'd see."

"I know," she said and slid down in her seat.

In other words, they were going to see his father.

TWO HOURS LATER, they'd met Ella the cat, loved her, and arranged to pick her up the day of Marcie and Mark's return from Hawaii. In exchange for the courtesy, Jennifer had spent some time with the breeder, examining some of the cats.

Another two hours later, and they were on the road, not far from where Bobby's father lived. Shades of yellow and orange painted the sky, the sun in steady decline, when Bobby pulled down a dirt road, which she assumed led to "Joey's Garage." Joey being Bobby's father.

They'd talked nonstop during the drive toward their visit with Ella—about her clinic and his time in the Army, at least what he was allowed to share. But since getting in the car, heading toward his father's place, he'd been tight-lipped.

Suddenly, they were parked between several large oak trees, not a building in sight, and Bobby killed the engine. "Why are we stopping?"

"I want to show you something," he said, popping open his door and motioning with his head for her to exit.

Jennifer joined him at the front of the car, fields of high grass mixed with yellow and purple flowers all around them. It was private, quiet, romantic.

Bobby threaded his fingers through hers. "This was one of my favorite places when I was a kid. I'd come here to get out of the house."

"To get away from your father," she said.

"He was always at the garage or the bar. I just liked this place. I used to bring my radio and books, and spend hours here." He walked backward and led her around one of the big oak trees. "This is what I wanted to show you." He turned her to face the tree and stepped behind her, his arms wrapping around her from behind. There, at the center of the tree's trunk, was a big heart carved with two lovers' names and a year, 1947.

Bobby nuzzled her neck. "This was some young couple's secret spot. Now it can be ours. I always wanted to bring you here, but I didn't want to explain why I didn't want to take you to see my father."

Jennifer's heart swelled with the confession, and she

rotated around in his arms, her hands sliding around his neck. She didn't miss the importance of a gesture that reached far beyond romance. He wouldn't have taken her before, but he would now. The boundaries were coming down.

"I'm glad you brought me today," she said, pressing to her toes and kissing him.

His hand molded her lower back, his tongue sweeping against hers in a lush stroke just before he nipped her lip. "We should carve the tree with our names," he suggested.

She laughed, feeling like a schoolgirl, and loving it. "All right," she said. "But you have to do all the work." She ran her hand over his bicep. "I'll watch all your delicious muscles flexing and make ooh and ahh sounds at all the right moments."

He kissed her, a short, firm kiss filled with a sexy reprimand. "Don't tease me," he warned, his voice that low hum that rattled through her nerves with sensual delight. "Or I might just have to take you right here against the tree."

Feeling playful, she taunted him, "I wonder if the couple who carved their names here before us tried the tree?"

A low growl escaped his lips. "You're naughty."

"You bring it out in me," she purred, nipping his lips as he had hers. "Only I think I'd rather be naughty on a blanket, which we don't have."

"Where's your sense of adventure?" he asked, his hand sliding over her backside and pressing her into his obvious erection.

"Waiting for a blanket," she assured him, and noting the fast encroaching darkness, added, "and candles. Let's carve our names before it gets dark."

Reluctantly, Bobby let her go. "Next time we'll bring a blanket."

The "next time" reference pleased Jennifer. It gave her hope that despite his reluctance to see his father, he really wasn't expecting his father to impact their future. "Do we even have a way to carve our names now?"

Bobby reached into his boot and pulled out a pocketknife. "A soldier is always prepared," he said, holding it up. He then produced a small penlight. "Let there be light."

Fifteen minutes later, the sun all but gone, Jennifer held the light on the tree as Bobby finished the carving. "Done," he said, flipping the knife shut and sliding it back in his boot.

"We'll have to come back when we can see it properly," she said, shining the light around the tree. "But at least we've marked our territory."

Bobby pushed to his feet and eased her upward with him, his body cradling hers. "The whole idea gives me the sudden urge to forget the blanket and claim you, not the territory." He leaned against the tree and molded her across the long, hard length of his hips and thighs.

She stared up at him, searching the hard lines of his face, obscured by shadows, sensing a shift in him—his mood darker, the playfulness of earlier gone.

His mouth closed down over hers, his lips firm, his tongue ruthless in its invasion, its demand. His hand, forceful as it guided her hips to his, his erection thick where it rested against her stomach.

Jennifer moaned into his mouth, tasting that darkness she sensed in him, the primitive lust—feeling it in his touch. On some level, in some place in her mind, Jennifer knew this was the beginning of a firestorm of more than passion. This was a foreshadowing of what was to come—of Bobby dealing with why he'd left, why he'd returned. She told herself to pull away. Knew she should ask questions, demand to understand what had caused his mood. If only she had asked questions seven years ago.

But now he was touching her, her bra unhooked, his hands everywhere. Gliding over her rib cage, gently brushing the curve beneath her breast. She moaned, arching into him, moaned as his hand slid under her shirt, cupping her breasts, pinching her nipples. She was wet, achy, ready to say to heck with a blanket.

For a few minutes, she didn't fight the drugging kisses or the enticement of his hands on her body. Jennifer was lost. Lost to kissing Bobby. Lost to his touch. Lost to the need to touch. Her hand slid over his crotch, over the bulge of his cock. She wanted him inside her. Oh, yes, inside her. Here, now.

A low, feral growl escaped his lips as she stroked his cock with her hand, spearing his tongue into her mouth. And it was the kiss—the wild, dark quality of Bobby's kiss that pierced the passion, bled into her soul. Called out to her in warning. She was losing him again. He was going to hurt her. Again. Hurt her again. Somehow, her palms steadied on his arms, and she shoved away, tearing her mouth from his.

"No," she gasped. "Stop." She squeezed her eyes shut against the scream of her body telling her to "go," not "stop." She forced her eyes open. "What is it, Bobby?" she rasped, her throat thick with desire, barely recognizable as her own. "What's wrong?"

The twinkling stars were barely seeping through the tree limbs, casting a reflection on his face.

"Nothing," he said, his hand sliding along her hip and tempting her to forget her objections. "The idea of taking you in the wilderness turns me on, is all." He leaned down and kissed her forehead, the edge about him beginning to fade. "Let's go see my father, so I can properly satisfy my craving—in your bed for now. We'll come back to the wilderness."

Nothing was wrong. But something *was* wrong. He knew it and so did she. They'd marked the tree with their names, but not with a guarantee of happiness.

CARVING THEIR NAMES in that tree with Jennifer had been the moment he'd made the incontrovertible decision—he was not going to reenlist. He was going to spend the rest of his life finding places like this one to share with Jennifer. No more traveling to a different country at the blink of an eye, barely remembering his real name, forgetting a holiday, forgetting his birthday. Missing Jennifer's. No more blood all the damn time. He was ready to be done with the blood. Especially that of men he considered friends. But Jennifer wasn't convinced. He could see it in her eyes. She didn't believe he was staying. She *wasn't* ready to give him her trust. Which brought to the surface the bitter reality of seeing his father, refusing to let him forget why he'd enlisted in the first place. And so he'd wanted to find a way to forget, to bury himself inside Jennifer under that tree—their tree—and forget visiting his father. Forget the past. Instead, Bobby was remembering all too well. He had to remember, he had to embrace what was, to find what could be. To prove to Jennifer he was worth the risk of opening her heart again.

He parked at the side of Joey's Garage, not about to announce his arrival. Streetlights and exterior lighting illuminated the area, but not the darkness of dread. He'd face his father on his own terms. And considering he preferred a "never" time frame to the apparent immediate one, that wasn't going so well.

Only yesterday he'd believed Jennifer had a right to see what he might become. Now, it was all he could do not to turn to Jennifer and remind her he wasn't his father, that he had simply let a toxic relationship press his buttons, or maybe he needed to remind himself.

"I've met him before," Jennifer said softly, as if she'd read his mind.

"You met him, yes," Bobby said, turning to her, "but it was brief and you got lucky. He was half sober and in a good mood."

Jennifer squeezed his hand. "I've dealt with Marcie's prewedding mood swings for weeks now. I can take your father for a short visit."

"All right," Bobby said. "But don't say I didn't warn you."

She reached for her door. "Ready?"

He reached for her, his fingers around her neck, kissing her. He drank in the flavor of her, the sweetness that was so her, the sweetness that gave him a reason to face the bitterness of his father.

Long moments later, he forced himself to draw back, the taste of her lingering on his tongue, his voice firm with resolve. "Now I'm ready." Bobby had every intention of proving that to Jennifer. And to himself.

17

JENNIFER ROUNDED THE front of the car to meet Bobby at the hood and stopped dead in her tracks as the sound of a low growl met her ears. She grabbed Bobby's arm. "Stop."

"I heard it," he said, a second before a Doberman pinscher lunged toward them snarling and barking, teeth bared. Big teeth on an angry dog.

"Don't move," Jennifer said, her heart in her throat. "Anything we do to seem aggressive will make it attack." The dog jumped forward and barked some more. "Of course, it might attack anyway."

"Considering you're a vet," Bobby said, his voice calm, unaffected, almost amused, as if he'd faced far worse than an enraged Doberman, "now seems a good time to ask if you'll be betting on me or the dog in the event a fight should ensue? Because if anyone is going to bite you, it's me, and it'll come with a heavy dose of pleasure. Fido here isn't going to get a chance to bite you." The dog snarled as if it resented the name. Bobby arched a brow. "Okay, I guess the name Fido isn't macho enough to suit you. Kujo it is." His gaze remained on Kujo. "What's the answer, Jen. Me or the dog?"

"I might be a vet," Jennifer said, amazed at how calm Bobby was because she was ready to crawl under the car, "but I wouldn't like being ripped apart by a dog any more than you would."

"Ripped apart is rather dramatic, sweetheart," he said. "You know something I don't?"

"I know I wish I didn't smell like cat right now, and that dog is going to attack if we don't do something and do it fast," she said, all too familiar with the look in its eyes.

"Well, well, well," came a countrified female voice. "Look what the dog drug up. Heel, girl." The dog snarled once more and backed away, sauntering over to stand by the woman who stroked its head. "Good girl, Dixie." The dog panted and glowed, a happy pet, rather than a killer.

Jennifer's gaze lifted to the brassy redhead in cutoff shorts and a T-shirt with cowboy boots, and long, lean legs that any girl would kill for. But her tanned face with fine lines gave away her age.

"My God," Jennifer said. "It's Marcie in twenty years."

"Kate?" Bobby said.

"Hell, yeah, boy," she said. "Who else you know who'd put up with your father?"

"Who's Kate?" Jennifer asked, confused.

"His stepmother," Kate said, kicking up the dirt as she headed for Bobby. "Who wants a hug!"

"Stepmom?!" Jennifer asked, confused.

Kate gave Bobby a big hug. "I thought I was going to have to go to Russia or Iraq or some crazy place to hunt you down. Don't you know how to call or visit?" She pursed her lips. "Never mind. Of course, I know why you didn't." She eyed Jennifer. "I'm guessing this young lady had something to do with you coming now."

"This is Jennifer, Kate," Bobby said, wrapping his arm around Jennifer and went on to explain to Jennifer, "Kate used to be my stepmother."

"Still am," Kate said. "I left the drunk SOB fifteen years ago because he was impossible to live with. Never divorced him." She grinned. "So I figured I better kick his ass and keep him."

Jennifer turned in Bobby's arms, excited at the discovery. Expecting the same from him. Instead she found a troubled, solemn look on his face.

"He's been sober three hundred and three days today, Bobby boy," Kate said. "Surely you got my letters."

He scrubbed his jaw. "I've been away on several long missions, back-to-back. I haven't checked my mail in a few months."

Kate made a "tsk" sound. "Come inside and holler at your father. He's going to be tickled you're here." She started walking. "Come, Dixie." The dog fell into step with Kate.

Bobby hung back, a stunned look on his face. Jennifer turned to him. "This is good, right?"

"Kate being back, telling me my father is sober and 'tickled' to see me is an alternative reality. I think I'm going to wake up any minute."

Jennifer smiled and laced her arm with his. "Let's go see your father."

Arm in arm, they strolled into the garage, an old Camaro in the docking area that Jennifer guessed to be from the seventies. Kate stood beside it. "Come out of there, Joey. I got someone for you to see."

"Tell 'em to hold their horses," came a grumble from beneath the car. "I almost got this. Oh, well, hell. I need a socket wrench."

Bobby stepped forward and grabbed a socket wrench from a metal table and bent down beside his father. "Here you go, Pops," he said.

Silence. Then, Joey Evans slid out from under the car in mechanics overalls, his gray hair cut close to his scalp, his eyes wide. "Bobby?" And then he was standing up, hugging his son. For a moment, Bobby was stiff, unmoving. His father held on tight anyway. "I'm sorry, son. I'm sorry for everything."

Jennifer's gaze met Kate's, and they were both crying. Father and son had found each other, and two loves had been reunited. In that instant, Jennifer wasn't sure she could be happier.

Bobby's father leaned back and patted his son's shoulder. "Let's go have a drink to celebrate." He gave a two-second pause in which Bobby must have grimaced, because his father chuckled and said, "A Coca Cola boy. There's not a beer in this great state of Texas, or beyond, worth losing my son over again."

"Coca Cola is Joey's replacement vice for beer," Kate explained. "One I happily supply."

Joey glanced over his son's shoulder at Kate, opening his mouth to respond, but instead, fixing his gaze on Jennifer. "Well, I'll be damned. Jennifer Jones."

Jennifer's eyes went wide. "You remember me?"

"Of course, I remember the woman my son planned to marry and give me grandbabies with," he said. "I was an ass when I was drinking but I never forgot a darn thing. Though I'd like to forget the part about being an ass."

Jennifer gaped at his directness and Bobby's arm slid to her back, a silent apology.

"We'd like to forget you were an ass, too," Kate assured him. "But you keep opening that big mouth of yours. Good thing you mean well." She glanced at Jennifer. "And he does."

"Oh, heck," Joey said, scrubbing his jaw, looking genuinely upset. "I didn't mean that in a bad way. I meant I'm glad you're still around."

Jennifer ignored the magnetic pull of Bobby, willing her to look at him, and the loosely used term *still around,* and graciously replied, "I'm flattered you remember me."

Kate seemed to sense the need to redirect the conversation and motioned toward the door. "Let's go inside and catch up on things. The place is messy, but it's home."

Quite some time later, Jennifer sat at a wooden table in the dining area overlooking the living room, where she eagerly consumed every detail of Bobby's old family home, from the wood paneling, old carpet and worn furniture, she could manage. That and her weight in the chocolate cookies Kate had baked earlier that day.

Jennifer brushed crumbs from her hands. "Those were so good. I have to stop before I eat as many as Bobby did." He'd eaten at least six. She'd managed to down four herself, but she was only admitting to three.

"I went to work at a bakery after I left Joey," she said. "Never thought I was the baking type but it was a job and I needed one. Next thing I knew, I loved it. I'm thinking about opening a little place of my own."

"Based on these cookies, I'd say it would be a success," Jennifer said. "I think I might need lessons."

"Better yet," she said, "you and Bobby come and let me cook for you. It'll do Joey's heart good. And mine, too."

"I'll do my best," Jennifer said, her gaze drifting to where Bobby, and his father, were looking at photo albums and talking—Joey more than Bobby—but they were talking. Healing had begun. Unbidden, sadness washed over Jennifer. She couldn't go making dinner plans with Kate. After Marcie and Mark's wedding was over, she didn't know when, or even if, she'd see Bobby again. For all she knew, something would trigger that flight mechanism in Bobby all over again, and he'd be gone.

Kate's hand covered Jennifer's where it rested on the table. "That man isn't going anywhere without you," she said softly, as if she'd read Jennifer's mind. "I can see it in his eyes when he looks at you." She patted Jennifer's hand and leaned back, speaking louder, as if she wanted Bobby to hear. "That doesn't mean Bobby doesn't need a good butt kicking like his father now and then. But I have a feeling you are up for the job."

Jennifer grinned. She liked Kate's feisty personality more with each passing minute.

Two hours later, Jennifer and Kate watched Joey tear up as he hugged his son goodbye. "I'm proud of you, Bobby Evans," he murmured softly, but not so much that Jennifer and Kate didn't hear. Then Joey stared Bobby in the eye. "And if you don't stay in touch, I swear I'll come find you—I don't care what kind of godforsaken jungle you're in. Understood?"

Bobby nodded. "Understood, Pops."

When Jennifer and Bobby pulled onto the highway, the silence inside the dark car was damning. "This was good, yes?" she prodded. "Your father is doing great, and Kate is wonderful."

"Yes," he said, his eyes glued to the road.

Yes. Nothing more. Jennifer sat there, contemplating pushing him to talk. Even sober, his father had triggered this, which seemed to prove her worst fear. His father had always been an excuse to walk away. It was always going to end like this, with Bobby finding some reason to shut her out again.

When they finally pulled up outside her condo, Bobby killed the engine, but not her whirlwind of emotions. She was clinging to a thread of composure. They sat there in silence for long seconds before Bobby said, "Jennifer—"

"Good night, Bobby," she said, pushing open her door, all too aware that just the sound of his voice, the anticipation of what he would say, was cracking her fragile shell. She didn't want to cry; she didn't want to yell. She just wanted away.

She was at the door in a flash, her hand shaking as she struggled with the keys. Suddenly, Bobby was there, big, warm, overpowering. His arms closed around her from behind, and he gently helped her unlock the door.

"I'm sorry," he whispered. "I didn't mean to upset you."

Jennifer squeezed her eyes shut, and for a few seconds, she allowed herself to revel in the feel of him holding her. Of the familiar warmth, strength, comfort. And yes, even passion. But she knew it was short-term. She knew he'd promise more and give her what he'd given her in the car. Withdrawal. And she couldn't do it. She couldn't live through it again.

"You wouldn't even talk to me in the car," she said, her voice hoarse with emotion. "Let me go, Bobby."

"I'm not letting you go ever again," he said and before she knew his intention, she was in the door and it was shut. He held her tightly in his arms. He repeated his words. "I'm not letting you go."

"You don't have to," she said. "I am. I'm letting go."

He ground his teeth until a muscle flexed in his jaw, steely silence, raw torment in his gaze that reached inside her and twisted and had her adding, "You shut me out again."

"I am trying to make sense of the past seven years," he said. "I left you. I left him. It took Kate to save him. That's a lot to swallow."

"I could tell you, you might not have been able to save him. The timing and the right person make all the difference. But I'm not the right person for you, Bobby. I'm the one you shut out."

"No," he said. "I'm not ready to say goodbye. You still owe me one night." He gave her a quick kiss and then he was gone.

Jennifer couldn't move; her mind spun with the implications of his words. One more night. One. Not two. Not a week. Not a lifetime. One. He'd agreed all too easily. That shouldn't surprise her. She'd seen how he'd pulled away over his father, how he still struggled with the past. And as much as she wanted Bobby, she didn't want him halfway. He was either in this or not. Obvious the "not" had the win here. But if he expected, after all she'd been through, to choose their final night, he had another think coming. "Damn you, Bobby," she whispered. "You don't get to decide when we say goodbye this time. Not this time." Somehow, she was going to do this on her terms.

18

THE FOLLOWING DAY, dressed in a navy silk chiffon dress, Jennifer rushed to the private banquet room in the restaurant hosting Marcie and Mark's rehearsal dinner. With the rehearsal complete, the wedding party would arrive any minute, and she still needed to place the bride and groom's gifts by the seating arrangement cards. She opened the double doors to the scent of lilacs, which adorned the center of the solid oak rectangular tables set in a U-shape. Removing the gifts from the bag on her shoulder, Jennifer rushed from seat to seat, carefully placing them in the proper locations.

She tried not to think about Bobby, who she hadn't heard from all week. He'd left, Marcie had said, to return the night before the wedding, which was tonight.

Jennifer had willed herself to ask nothing more, and Marcie hadn't volunteered any information. But Marcie knew something; Jennifer had seen it in her eyes. Ah— but Marcie and Bobby had years of secrets. All of which Jennifer had been excluded from. Nothing had changed. Nothing was ever going to change with Bobby.

She'd tried her hardest to tell herself she didn't care.

Which apparently required pulling extra hours at the clinic to avoid thinking herself insane, because she'd worked plenty of hours this past week.

Today though, she'd spent with helping Marcie and her mother, Sharon—who unlike Kate was tall with a short, blond spiky do—prepare for tonight and the wedding the next day.

Jennifer was halfway around the tables when she froze at the sight of a seating card with "Bobby Evans" on it.

"You didn't expect me, I guess?"

His voice, oh, his voice. Why did Bobby's voice have to be so deep and sexy? Why did it have to stroke her inside out and send chills down her spine?

She inhaled a discreet, relaxing breath and then lifted her gaze to his, noting the black suit and white shirt with a navy-blue tie that matched her dress. Either he'd asked Marcie what Jennifer was wearing or he'd taken a guess based on her love of that color. Either way, it wasn't scoring him any points after days of silence. He did silence too damn well.

"You aren't part of the wedding party," she commented, and moved forward to set the next gift by a place setting.

Bobby let the door shut behind him. His blond hair was longer than she remembered, his blue eyes glistening with sensuality. "Mark made me an honorary best man for keeping everyone out of jail. It seemed to leave a *lasting impression*."

Oh, now, that made her mad. She turned away from him and started putting out the rest of her gifts. She was out of time anyway.

He laughed. "No comment?"

She cut him a look. "No," she said lightly. "No comment."

"You aren't going to ask where I've been?"

Mad again. Oh, so mad. She didn't answer. Couldn't answer. Not yet. "No, I am not. In fact…"

Jennifer set the last gift in its place, and picked up her name card that was next to Bobby's—no doubt, by Marcie's doing. She then walked to the other side of the table, snagged someone else's name card, and replaced it with hers. Jennifer returned to the seat beside Bobby's and set the new place card down. "There. Now we don't have to make conversation at all."

The doors behind him burst open as a slew of guests overwhelmed the room. Bobby faded into the crowd, and she wished he would fade from her awareness. No matter who she mingled with, no matter what she did, Jennifer could feel Bobby close, feel him watching her, feel him as if he were touching her.

Soon, they were all seated and chatting, and Bobby sat, much to her chargin, directly across from her. How—*how*—had he managed that little trick?

Every cell of her body felt Bobby's presence. Even her wine tasted of him, sin and satisfaction. She sipped it, allowing the waiter to take her salad plate when her gaze caught on the waitress across the table leaning in close to Bobby. Flirting. He laughed at something she said, and Jennifer felt her nerves prickle and turn to fire.

Abruptly, Bobby's gaze lifted and caught on Jennifer's, his eyes narrowing far too intuitively, as if he sensed the edge crackling off her. Her hand tightened on her wineglass in an effort to keep it steady as she lowered it to the table with slow care. She would not be jealous. She was not jealous.

The waitress leaned down and said something else to Bobby, and Jennifer pushed to her feet, and headed toward the hallway. A fast detour to her right, and she was down the stairwell leading to the private, single-stall restroom she'd found earlier that night. She shoved open the door and pushed inside, but the temporary relief of privacy faded as Bobby tugged her back into the hallway. Jennifer was caught between his big body and the door.

THANKFUL FOR THE STAIRWELL that offered privacy, Bobby's hands settled on Jennifer's waist. Did she really think he'd let her run away? Of course, she didn't know he'd spent the past few days working on a plan to ensure she knew he was here to stay. But she would. Soon.

"What do you think you are doing?" she asked, her voice low, full of demand.

"You were jealous," he accused.

"I was not jealous!" she insisted.

"I went to high school with that waitress, Jen," he said, noting the flush on Jennifer's cheeks. The fullness of her kissable bottom lip quivered ever-so-slightly. "There was no flirting. Just reminiscing."

"Oh, there was flirting," she said, and looked instantly as if she regretted the statement, her fingers curling into her palms.

He arched a brow. "So you *were* jealous?"

"No!"

His lips twitched. "I wasn't flirting," he promised. "Except with you."

She pressed her hand to his chest. "I don't want to hear this."

"Well, I need you to hear it," he countered. "I need you to know there is no other woman that matters and I won't let you create one to run away from me." He lowered his voice. "From us." He leaned closer, inhaling her scent. "You owe me a night. You promised."

She drew back, her hand falling from his chest and almost returning before she caught herself. "You can't be serious."

"I couldn't be more serious," he said, molding her closer, and bringing her hand back to his chest in the process. Warmth seeped through his skin, scorching him.

"I did not," she said. "You don't get to decide when we see each other, and when we don't. You don't come and go as you please. I told you. I'm done."

Footsteps sounded and then, "Jennifer?" Marcie stopped dead halfway down the stairs. "Whoops. Didn't mean to interrupt. I was just worried about you two."

Jennifer glared at Bobby. "Let me go."

Bobby stared down at her, trying to decide if he really wanted to do that.

Marcie cleared her throat. "Ah…no rush. I'll just head back to the table."

"I'm coming with you," Jennifer said quickly.

Bobby pressed his forehead to hers, and spoke in a low voice. "Marcie needs you tonight," he said. "But I need you, too." He stepped back, but not without claiming her hand again. "I'm going to show you how much, Jen. Tomorrow, after the wedding. I promise."

BOTH IN THEIR pj's, ready for the before-the-wedding slumber party of two, Jennifer tried to coax Marcie into sleep. "It's no sleep that makes your eyes puffy, Marc. You need to sleep, and you're wound up like the Energizer bunny."

Marcie just pursed her lips, eyes wide open. Meanwhile, Jennifer sat down in the chair she and Bobby had shared the night of the party, trying to forget how good lying there in his arms had felt.

"I can't believe it's tomorrow," Marcie said and reached for her cell phone.

"Please," Jennifer said. "*Do not* check your messages *again*."

"What if—"

"The wedding planner calls?" Jennifer finished. "The phone would ring. We're right here."

Marcie crossed then recrossed her legs and set her phone down. "I'm making you crazy."

"No," Jennifer replied. "You're making you crazy. I'm fine. After all—I have a broken heart and a lime dress." She rolled her eyes and said at the same time as Marcie, "Yellow-green." Jennifer glowered. "Not a color. Looked it up in the dictionary."

"Fine," Marcie said. "It's lime, but I enjoyed making you say yellow-green. That whole 'bride has the power' thing."

"Only I never said yellow-green," she reminded her.

"No," Marcie said, and snickered. "But the other girls did. So did the wedding planner."

Jennifer laughed. "Oh, you are bad, Marcie."

"Yeah," she said, scooting to the headboard to lean against it. "Mark was in on the joke. He thought it was pretty funny, but then, he gets my bizarre sense of humor." She sat back up. "I'm so nervous."

"Calm down," Jennifer instructed, plumping pillows.

"Okay, so distract me from my wedding nerves and tell me about the hot, welcome-back sex that you and Bobby have had the last week," she said.

"Welcome back? Right. He comes and goes without a word, and I'm supposed to keep welcoming him back with sex? I don't think so."

Marcie studied Jennifer a long while. "Did you ask where he was?"

"Do you know?"

"No," she said. "But Bobby is Special Forces. If he could have told you where he went, I'm sure he would have."

"He could have told me he had a work situation," she said.

"Are you sure?" Marcie asked. "Maybe he was forbidden. Look, Jen, you and Bobby saved our party. Then, you turned around and saved our wedding. You gave us another chance. You're good together."

But they *weren't* together. They were always apart. And even when they were together, she would always wonder when he'd be gone. She eyed Marcie. "Go to sleep, hon. Tomorrow, you are going to marry the man of your dreams." And Jennifer was going to say a final farewell to hers.

19

THE WEDDING DAY WAS HECTIC, but the weather was beautiful, the church perfect aside from the fact that her mother caught the flu and her father wouldn't be present to make Bobby squirm. Of course, her father liked Bobby, so why give Bobby a chance to win him over again? Aside from the Bobby situation, Marcie was a wreck, and her mother wasn't much better. And as they neared the fifteen-minute mark before the big event, Jennifer tried to be the calming force in the dressing room. She was failing miserably.

"My shoes," Marcie said, a hint of hysteria in her voice. "I can't find my shoes."

"Hold on, dear," her mother said, looking tall and elegant in a fitted, pale green suit dress, her voice pretending her normal coolness when she was anything but. Still she added confidently, "I'll find them."

The next thing Jennifer knew, the room was awash in lime-green, frantic females as the shoes were nowhere to be found.

"Oh, my God!" Marcie screamed. "I left them on my bed!"

Sharon and the bridal party all gasped in unison. Jennifer squeezed her eyes shut.

"My shoes!" Marcie screamed.

"Her shoes!" Sharon screamed, no longer maintaining her facade of cool.

The girls began a rumble of worried chatter.

"Everyone out!" Jennifer said, her lashes snapping open. "Go to the next room. Marcie needs calm." Good grief, Jennifer needed calm. And the night of no sleep, as she replayed every last second with Bobby these past two weeks, did not help. Nor did knowing she was going to see him any minute.

Everyone stared at Jennifer, as if shocked that she'd dared demand they leave. Sharon piped in, "Go! Mother has spoken."

The girls quickly turned obedient and rushed to the connecting dressing room, pulling the door shut.

Jennifer straightened, running her hand over the formfitting, lime-green silk of her knee-length dress and hoping it traveled well. "I'll go get the shoes."

"There's no time," Marcie said frantically, her veil whisking behind her as she began to pace.

"Stop pacing," Sharon reprimanded. "You'll mess up the hem of your dress."

Marcie whirled on her mother, brushing a red ringlet gently back from her brow, her veil already in place. "I have no shoes, Mother. There's no time to get the shoes."

"I'll make it in time," Jennifer insisted. "And if we start five minutes late, who cares?"

"That's right," Sharon said. "Who cares!"

"I'm going," Jennifer said, rushing forward and starting to hug Marcie and then stopping in her tracks.

"Okay. Pretend I hugged you and was really supportive. I don't want to mess anything up."

"Hurry, Jen," Marcie said. "Please hurry."

Jennifer was already grabbing the necessary keys, and heading to the door. "And don't get anything on your dress!" Marcie called.

Right, Jennifer thought. No problem. It wasn't like she was having a rash of clumsiness or anything. She rushed out into the hallway and cut past the connected hall where the men were dressing. Bobby's voice rumbled in the air as a door opened, and she caught a quick glimpse of blond hair and broad shoulders in his honorary best man tuxedo.

Her heart skipped a beat as she hit the red exit button on the side of the door and pushed the lever. Only it didn't open. She hit the button again, her gaze lifting to find Bobby headed in her direction, those long legs carrying him toward her far too quickly.

"Jennifer," he called.

"Gotta go!" she said. "Errand for the bride." She shoved the bar on the door, and this time it opened for her. She rushed away. She was on a quest for shoes, not Bobby. Never Bobby. Always Bobby. Damn him.

She rushed across the paved parking lot and cringed. Someone had blocked her car. No. No! This wasn't happening.

"I thought only the bride and groom ran away at the altar," Bobby asked from behind her.

Another squeeze-your-eyes-shut moment followed, this time with the added bonus of heat pooling low in her stomach at the sound of the man's voice.

She inhaled and turned, trying hard not to show the crushing heat in her chest at the gloriously sexy way he filled out his tuxedo. "I need a ride. As in now. Marcie left her shoes at her house."

Those twinkling blue eyes turned worried. "What are you waiting for? Let's go." He yanked his keys from his pocket and motioned her to the right. To a pickup truck. An F150 like he'd said he had back at the base.

Jennifer stopped dead in her tracks. "You're in that truck?"

His eyes lit with challenge. "I told you I drive an F150."

A funny feeling swelled in her chest. "How'd it get here?"

"I drove it," he said and arched a brow. "Now. Don't we need those shoes?"

Shaking herself, Jennifer started forward. "Yes. Shoes." She headed for the passenger's side of the truck. Bobby followed and unlocked it automatically. It was high. Her dress was snug at the knees, and pulling it up would wrinkle it.

"Need help?" Bobby asked, a second before his arms were around her, scooping her up and carefully setting her in the truck.

Oh, God. He made her feel delicate and protected. Jennifer didn't want to depend on Bobby and have him be gone, but having him come to her rescue now felt so darn good.

His hand settled on her thigh, his eyes alight with male appreciation. "I wouldn't want your dress to get messed up. Especially when you make it look so good." The next thing she knew he was shutting the door of the truck and rushing to the driver's side.

He climbed into the truck and started the engine. They were on the main road in seconds. "I guess Marcie needed one last wedding disaster before the big moment," he said, chuckling. The sound was rich and masculine, and Jennifer found herself laughing as well.

"Yes," she agreed. "I'll need a honeymoon to recover from Marcie's wedding." Too late she realized her misstep and she gulped.

"Where," he said, casting her a teasing smile, "would you want to go for this honeymoon?"

"I didn't mean honeymoon," she corrected, her heart about to explode right out of her chest. "I meant vacation."

"Semantics," he said.

"It is not," she said and bit back another word. He was baiting her, and in her heart, she wanted it to be for all the right reasons. But she was scared. "Is the truck supposed to convince me you're here to stay? And don't tell me you got out of the Army. Well, you can always go back in with a simple Dear Jen letter."

He gave an incline of his head and turned down Mark and Marcie's street, which was thankfully, not far from the church.

"All right. I won't tell you I got out of the Army." He turned into the driveway.

Okay. She couldn't breathe. "Did you?"

He smiled. "You told me not to tell you." He popped the door of his truck open. "Stay here and protect your dress. Where are the shoes and keys?"

Keys. Keys. Where were the keys. "Purse," she said. "My purse." She grabbed it and handed him the keys. "Shoes are on the bed. I hope." His hand closed over the keys and caressed her fingers a moment too long. Had he gotten out? Had he?

He was gone, though, rushing across the lawn in long masculine strides that had her mouth going dry.

She sat there, her mind racing, fingers curled in her palms. Bobby was making her crazy. Her cell rang, and she dug it out of her purse, knowing it was Marcie without looking at caller ID.

"I'm at the house," Jennifer said. "Back in five minutes."

"Is Bobby with you, because word is, he left to get Mark a bottle of water and never came back."

Oh, damn. "Yes. My car was blocked in. He drove me."

"Okay," Marcie said with relief. "Okay. Everyone is accounted for."

Sharon spoke in the background.

"She's at the house," Marcie told her. "You said you're at the house, right, Jen?"

"Yes," she agreed, as Bobby rushed out of the house, shoebox in hand. "And we have the shoes."

"You're sure?" Marcie asked.

"Bobby's getting in the truck with them now," Jennifer assured her.

"You check the shoes," Marcie said. "Make sure they're the right ones."

Jennifer rolled her eyes and looked at Bobby. "She wants me to check them." He opened the box and Jennifer nodded her approval, before telling Marcie, "The shoes are secure. I repeat, Houston, the shoes are secure."

"Ha-ha," Marcie said. "Get your smart-ass back here!" She hung up. Jennifer tucked her phone back into her purse and zipped it.

"Hang on, sweetheart," he said, backing out of the driveway. "We have a shoe emergency."

Jennifer laughed at the craziness of the situation, as he skidded out of the driveway, and she clung to the door. A few minutes of traffic maneuvers followed before they were back at the church, with not a parking spot to be found. Bobby pulled to the side of the building.

"We're parking here," he announced.

Jennifer reached for her door.

"Don't even think about it," he said, gently shackling her arm. "Think about the dress."

And then he was around the truck, opening her door and scooping her up. He set her down, sliding her down carefully, and reached around her, his body brushing hers, awareness driving her insane.

He handed her the shoes, his blue eyes dancing. "I'll see you in the church."

Jennifer raced toward the door, and Sharon greeted her. Sharon snatched the shoes and started to run, as if the shoes were Marcie's life support. Then, with an apparent second thought, she turned back and grabbed Jennifer's hand. "Come on! You're the maid of honor."

A few minutes of pure chaos ensued until finally the wedding party lined up at the front of the crowded church as Mark and Marcie said their vows. Bobby, though he hadn't walked the aisle, stood with the groomsmen, his eyes holding hers, unspoken words swimming between them.

This could have been them. But it wasn't. And Jennifer couldn't let herself forget that. She'd worked hard to build a life. She couldn't let Bobby inside that world and then have him disappear again. She loved him too much to endure that pain again.

Standing there, wanting him, needing him, she felt the emptiness inside her as she thought of what might have been between her and Bobby. She tore her gaze from Bobby's. She'd built a good life. She didn't want to live fearful over when Bobby would leave again. She wouldn't let him hurt her again.

THERE WAS CAKE and presents. There was happiness. An hour and a half after the ceremony, the reception was in full-blown, party mode at a building adjacent to an art gallery in downtown Austin, complete with a gorgeous courtyard for pictures.

And there were pictures. Lots of pictures. After the "final" shots with the bride, the groom and the best man, Jennifer was ready for retreat. Especially considering she was oh-so-aware of Bobby nearby, their gazes randomly colliding, her heart skipping a beat each and every time.

"That's it," the photographer said, and Jennifer headed to the sidelines.

"Wait, Jennifer!" Marcie called out and turned to the photographer. "I have one more set of photos. Bobby! Where are you?"

Jennifer glared at Marcie and stormed to her side. "Are you nuts."

"I am perfectly, happily sane," she said. "Go take the photos. I'm the bride. Do as I say."

Jennifer glanced over her shoulder to find Bobby standing in photo position. She cast Marcie another glare and silently called her nasty names.

"Hey," Marcie said with reprimand. "Don't curse the bride on her wedding day."

"I didn't," Jennifer denied.

"Thinking counts," Marcie said and pointed to her head. "And I can hear you thinking." She pressed her hands to her hips. "Now. Go enjoy your man."

"He's not my man," Jennifer grumbled in a frustrated glower before whirling around to face Bobby. He arched a brow. She tilted her chin up and walked toward him. She could do this. Just a few more hours and this would be over.

Bobby slid his hand around her waist. "I missed you, too, sweetheart."

She turned to face him, forgetting the camera, despite the fact that it flashed. "You never stop, do you?"

He stepped closer. "Do you really want me to?"

No. Yes. No. And why did he have to smell so good? "I want—"

"Jennifer," the photographer called out, saving her, because she had no idea what she would have said. The photographer's instructions continued. "Put your hand on Bobby's upper arm and keep looking up at him exactly like you have been."

Jennifer did as ordered, every touch, every connection with his body, electric. And he knew it. His eyes smoldered with awareness.

"Perfect," the photographer declared. "Don't move."

"You look beautiful in that dress," he whispered.

"Stop, Bobby," she ordered.

"We're back to 'stop' again?"

"Yes," she hissed. "We're back to 'stop.' Behave."

"Turn and face forward," the photographer called out.

"Jennifer, in front. Bobby, behind her with your hands on her waist."

Bobby's eyes twinkled. "I'm betting he wants you to smile for this one."

She ground her teeth. "Behave." She faced forward.

Bobby framed her body with his, his hands settling on her shoulders as he leaned in and whispered, "But you like it when I misbehave."

"I do n—"

He nuzzled her neck and a shivery, aroused sensation rippled through her body. Jennifer's lashes lowered as the heat slid through, and for an instant, there was only Bobby.

"Now that's a picture!" the photographer yelled. "I think that's it. If the bride is happy."

"Oh, yes," Marcie said, wrapping her arm through Mark's. "I am, indeed, happy. And now it's time for the first dance. They're waiting for us."

Jennifer darted forward, out of Bobby's reach and didn't look back, weaving her way into the crowd and near the dance floor, but on the opposite side from the wedding party. She needed space. She eased into a chair, her legs wobbly.

Soon, Marcie and Mark were on the dance floor, in a lover's embrace. But it wasn't long until the music shifted to a fun country beat, and a mass of guests crowded in with them.

Jennifer was about to find some water, when she was tugged to her feet by Scott, the best man, and pulled to the dance floor, into the throng of dancers.

"No!" she yelled, but it was too late.

Scott grinned at her and pulled her in far too close.

"Everyone knows the best man and the maid of honor have to dance, and we didn't," he said, his hand a little too low on her back.

A slow song came on, and Jennifer knew she was in trouble.

"This is my dance," Bobby said, appearing by her side and towering over Scott by several inches. It wasn't just that Bobby was big. He wore confidence like a second skin. The kind you didn't have to announce or flaunt—it simply existed, and that made it, and him, all the more intimidating.

"No problem, Bobby man," Scott said, making a quick escape.

Jennifer did, too; she darted away, not about to be molded close to Bobby for a slow dance. She quickly worked through the crowd and found a quiet corner.

Bobby appeared and slid his hand in hers. "You promised me we'd go back to that spot I showed you. I intend for you to remember every last second of this night. Meet me at our tree at midnight."

A night with Bobby. Images of them naked, making passionate love, flickered in her mind and had her squeezing her thighs together. The idea of one last night—well, it was her heart squeezing on that one. She'd tried the big kiss-off nights before and failed. Now this?

She tilted her chin up. "We don't have a tree."

"The names carved in it say otherwise," he reminded her. "You owe me this. You owe *us* this." He leaned in closer and brushed his lips near her ear. "I'll bring a blanket." He kissed her neck, and then he was gone.

Several hours later, after Marcie had refused to throw the bouquet, handing it to Jennifer instead—with Bobby watching—Bobby was now nowhere to be found, and midnight was fast approaching. The bride and groom were gone. And it was time for Jennifer to decide. Was she going to lay her heart on the line and meet Bobby?

BOBBY STOOD UNDER THAT San Antonio tree, it's location significant in so many ways. It was the place he'd felt he'd finally conquered his demons. The place he hoped Jennifer had fallen in love with him again. Never as nervous, he surveyed his watch—it was five minutes after midnight. She wasn't coming. He'd been sure she'd come, sure she'd give them one last chance. And he'd planned. He'd changed into jeans and set the stage. A blanket on the ground, two lanterns and a few big surprises that he hoped would prove he planned to give her the world. But she wasn't here.

Five more minutes and he was pacing. Another five, and he was on the blanket, sitting down, defeated, staring at their names carved in the base of the tree. His hands slid into his hair, mentally kicking himself for shutting down on her in the car.

A flicker of light jerked his attention to the road. A car. The instant he was sure it was Jennifer, he started to stand, but thought better of it. Her tardiness said she'd hesitated to come here. He'd overwhelmed her or underwhelmed her, he had no idea which. He needed to take things slow, tread cautiously.

She pulled her car next to his truck and killed the lights. Long seconds passed and Bobby barely contained the urge to go after her. Finally, when he was about out of restraint, the door shoved open.

She walked to him, dressed in black jeans and a

T-shirt that blended with the night. She stopped at the edge of the trees for just an instant, as if stunned by the romantic setup he'd prepared. He hoped he'd pleased her.

At the edge of the blanket, she towered over him, her hands crossed in front of her. "Hi," she said softly.

"Hi," he said, aching to pull her into his arms. "I thought you weren't going to show up."

"I thought I wasn't going to show up," she said.

"But you did."

"Yes."

He patted the blanket. "Will you sit down with me?"

She shook her head. "No. I…I don't think I should stay. Bobby, all of this…it's great. You were always great. Always romantic. But…"

"I left," he said. "I know." It was all he could do to keep from reaching for her. "The other night when I went silent on you in the car, I wasn't shutting you out. I didn't know what I was feeling to put it into words. But I would have if you would have given me a little more time. I wanted nothing more than to hold you and figure out how to save us that night. I was beating myself up with what-ifs. But I would have talked to you. I will tonight. If you let me." He offered her his hand. "Sit down with me."

He could see her throat bob, her expression softening in the flickering lantern light. Slowly, she slid her hand to his and went down on the blanket to sit down facing him, her knees, like his, propped in front of her.

He reached out and touched her cheek. "After that night," he said, "seeing how easily you felt I was pulling away, I knew I had to do more than tell you I was serious about us. I knew I had to show you. And I knew you deserved to know what I was going to be, and do, when I got out of the Army. So I got to work. The first thing I did was fly back to base and sign my exit paperwork. I still have to go back for a week, but I'm done, out."

"You've been a soldier for seven years," she said. "I saw you save lives at the Hotzone. Don't get out for me, Bobby. It's not an either-or. It's not about that."

"I'd be gone all the time," he said. "It's no way to have a relationship."

"It's not about you being gone," she said. "Not for duty. It would be hard, but I would never make you choose."

"I know," he said. "But I'm choosing. I'm tired of death. I'm tired of not having a place to call home. I don't want to be gone all the time. So..." He reached to the side of the blanket and held up a set of keys.

"What's that?"

"I had money saved and I put it to use," he said. "I—we, I hope, are now co-owners of the Hotzone. Rocky was going to sell. I convinced him to bring on a partner instead. I'm hoping to convince the guys you met—Ryan and Caleb—to join us one day."

Her hand was on his leg now, her voice lifting, a hint of excitement. "You did this already? You invested?"

He nodded. "I did. And I called an Austin Realtor and asked her to send me over some lakeside properties for us to look through." He handed her a folder. "That dream house we wanted so many years ago, Jen."

She took the folder, her hand shaking as she thumbed through the pages, and then glanced up at him, her eyes glassy. "Bobby, I—"

"Wait," he said, kissing her hand and setting the folder on the blanket. "One more thing."

He pulled her to her feet and discreetly reached in his pocket before going down on his knee and taking her hand. He held up the ring he'd picked out only a few days before, a single stone as big as he could afford—simple and elegant, like her.

"Oh, wow," she whispered and started to cry.

"Jennifer. I love you. Make me a happy man and give me the chance to show you that, every day, for the rest of our lives. Please tell me I've convinced you I'm not going anywhere without you. Marry me, Jen. Be my wife."

"Yes," she said, going down on her knees to wrap her arms around his neck. "Yes. I love you, Bobby. I missed you so much."

He framed her face with his hands and wiped tears from her cheeks with his thumbs. This was the first time since he'd returned that she'd said either of those things to him without any sign of hesitation. "Do you know how good it is to hear you say you love me? Say it again."

"I love you, Bobby."

He kissed her and slid the ring on her finger.

"It's perfect," she said. "But just for the record, this doesn't mean I'm going to jump out of a plane."

Bobby pulled her down on the blanket. "You can jump, baby. Because I'm always going to be there to catch you. You have my word. Now, let's properly mark out our territory. We do have a blanket."

Epilogue

AFTER A WEEK of making love as many times as possible, shopping for a house, visiting her parents and, in general, falling in love all over again, Bobby and Jennifer stood in Marcie and Mark's kitchen behind the counter with a welcome-home cake for their arrival back from their honeymoon.

"Oh, how sweet!" Marcie screamed. She rushed forward and hugged Jennifer.

"I'll get the plates," Mark said. "The flight was long, and I'm starving."

Marcie surveyed Bobby. "You're still here. Should I assume you are now a civilian?"

Jennifer leaned in and wrapped her arm around his waist. "I decided to keep him. And…" She bent down and unlatched the cat cage that was hidden behind the counter. She lifted Ella. "And we're hoping you will keep our wedding gift and give her lots of love."

Marcie gasped and took the cat into her arms. "She's beautiful." She glanced over her shoulder. "Mark, isn't she beautiful?"

Mark smiled, love in his eyes, an appreciative look cast between Jennifer and Bobby.

Several minutes of spoiling the cat followed until Bobby said, "We hate to gift-and-run, but I have to be back on base for a week, and then Jennifer and I are flying out from there for a little trip."

Ella purred in Marcie's lap, and suddenly, Marcie noticed the ring. "You have a ring! A ring! Mark, they're getting married."

Jennifer could feel herself glowing. "Yes. Actually next week. On a beach in Mexico. Just the two of us."

Marcie argued about not being able to attend, but in the end, she hugged Jennifer and Bobby and begged for pictures. Jennifer and Bobby left shortly after, ready to begin their new life together, while Marcie and Mark learned how to take care of baby Ella.

Seven days later, Jennifer and Bobby stood barefoot on the sandy beach of a Mexico resort, the bluest water Jennifer had ever seen as the backdrop. Bobby wore a tuxedo, and Jennifer wore a long, formfitting white dress, with delicate embroidery. It was just the two of them, the preacher and a photographer. There was no music, no fancy frills. Only confessions of the heart. Simple romance, just how they wanted it. Of course, they'd had to promise the families a cake-tasting reception upon their return, which had an ever-growing invitation list. But for now, they had escaped into their own private world.

How Jennifer made it through the ceremony without crying, she didn't know. She could hardly believe that after all those years they'd been apart, she and Bobby had found their way back to each other. And finally, the preacher pronounced them "man and wife."

Bobby stared at Jennifer, love brimming from his eyes, and pulled her close. "You're everything to me,

Mrs. Evans." And then he kissed her. Jennifer cried then—happy tears, joyful tears—and since she'd never replaced her waterproof mascara, she was pretty sure she was going to look like a mess for her photos. But she was too happy to care. She had just married the man of her dreams and they had a lifetime to make perfect pictures.

* * * * *

HARLEQUIN® *Blaze*™

COMING NEXT MONTH

Available January 25, 2011

#591 NOT ANOTHER BLIND DATE...
Janelle Denison, Leslie Kelly, Jo Leigh

#592 BREAKING THE RULES
Uniformly Hot!
Tawny Weber

#593 TAKE MY BREATH AWAY...
The Wrong Bed
Cara Summers

#594 THE WILD CARD
Men Out of Uniform
Rhonda Nelson

#595 TURN UP THE HEAT
Checking E-Males
Isabel Sharpe

#596 HEAT OF THE MOMENT
It Takes a Hero
Karen Foley

REQUEST YOUR FREE BOOKS!

2 FREE NOVELS PLUS 2 FREE GIFTS!

HARLEQUIN®

Blaze™

Red-hot reads!

*Harlequin Romance author Donna Alward is loved
for her gorgeous rancher heroes.*

*Meet Wyatt as he's confronted by both a precious
little pink bundle left on his doorstep and his neighbor Elli
who's going to show him the ropes....*

Introducing
PROUD RANCHER, PRECIOUS BUNDLE

THE SQUAWKING QUIETED as Elli picked the baby up, and Wyatt turned around, trying hard to ignore the feelings of inadequacy as Darcy immediately stopped fussing.

"Maybe she's uncomfortable. What do you think, sweetheart?" Elli turned her conversation to the baby.

"What do you think is wrong?" Wyatt asked, putting the coffee pot back on the burner.

A strange look passed over Elli's face, one that looked like guilt and panic. But it was gone quickly. "I couldn't say," she replied.

"But you were so good with her this afternoon." Wyatt put his hands on his hips.

"Lucky, that's all. I just...remembered a few things." The same strange look flitted over her features once more.

Wyatt took the coffee to the table. "You fooled me. You looked like you knew exactly what you were doing." So much so that Wyatt had felt completely inept. A feeling he despised. He was used to being the one in control.

Elli and Darcy walked the length of the kitchen and back. After a few moments, she admitted, "I haven't really cared for a baby before. The things I thought of were simply things I'd heard about. Not from experience, Mr. Black."

Her chin jutted up, closing the subject but making him

want to ask the questions now pulsing through his mind. But then he remembered the old saying—*Don't look a gift horse in the mouth.* He'd benefit from whatever insight she had and be glad of it.

"I don't really know what babies need," he said. "I fed her, patted her back like you did, walked her to sleep, but every time I put her down…"

Wyatt almost groaned. Of course. He'd forgotten one important thing. He'd been so focused on getting the formula the right temperature that he'd forgotten to check her diaper. Not that he had any clue what to do there either.

Pulling calves and shoveling out stalls was far less intimidating than one tiny newborn.

"She's probably due for a diaper change, isn't she." He tried to sound nonchalant. This was a perfect opportunity. Elli must know how to change a diaper. He could simply watch her so he'd know better for the next time.

Instead, Elli came around the corner of the counter and placed Darcy back in his arms. "Here you go, Uncle Wyatt," she said lightly. "You get diaper duty. I'll fix the coffee. Cream and sugar?"

Oh boy, Wyatt thought, looking down into Darcy's pursed face, his smug plan blown to smithereens. He was in for it now.

Will sparks fly between Elli and Wyatt?

Find out in
PROUD RANCHER, PRECIOUS BUNDLE

Available February 2011 from Harlequin Romance

Try these Healthy and Delicious Spring Rolls!

INGREDIENTS

2 packages rice-paper
spring roll wrappers
(20 wrappers)

1 cup grated carrot

¼ cup bean sprouts

1 cucumber, julienned

1 red bell pepper, without
stem and seeds, julienned

4 green onions
finely chopped—
use only the green part

DIRECTIONS

1. Soak one rice-paper wrapper
   in a large bowl of hot water
   until softened.

2. Place a pinch each of carrots,
   sprouts, cucumber, bell
   pepper and green onion on the
   wrapper toward the bottom
   third of the rice paper.

3. Fold ends in and roll tightly
   to enclose filling.

4. Repeat with remaining
   wrappers. Chill before
   serving.

Find this and many more delectable recipes
including the perfect dipping sauce in

Silhouette® Desire

USA TODAY bestselling author

ELIZABETH BEVARLY

**is back with a steamy
and powerful story.**

Gavin Mason is furious and vows revenge on
high-price, high-society girl Violet Tandy.
Her novel is said to be fiction, but everyone
knows she's referring to Gavin as a client in
her memoir. The tension builds when they
learn not to judge a book by its cover.

THE BILLIONAIRE
GETS HIS WAY

*Available February
wherever books are sold.*

Always Powerful, Passionate and Provocative.

Visit Silhouette Books at www.eHarlequin.com

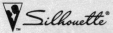

ROMANTIC
SUSPENSE

Sparked by Danger, Fueled by Passion.

NEW YORK TIMES BESTSELLING AUTHOR

RACHEL LEE

No Ordinary Hero

Strange noises...a woman's mysterious disappearance
and a killer on the loose who's too close for comfort.

With no where else to turn, Delia Carmody looks
to her aloof neighbour to help, only to discover
that Mike Windwalker is no ordinary hero.

Available in February.
Wherever books are sold.

Visit Silhouette Books at www.eHarlequin.com

SRS27709R2

HARLEQUIN Presents

USA TODAY bestselling author

Sharon Kendrick

introduces

HIS MAJESTY'S CHILD

The king's baby of shame!

King Casimiro harbors a secret—no one in the kingdom
of Zaffirinthos knows that a devastating accident has left
his memory clouded in darkness. And Casimiro himself
cannot answer why Melissa Maguire, an enigmatic English
rose, stirs such feelings in him…. Questioning his ability
to rule, Casimiro decides he will renounce the throne.
But Melissa has news she knows will rock the palace
to its core—*Casimiro has an heir!*

Law dictates Casimiro cannot abdicate, so he must find a
way to reacquaint himself with Melissa—his new queen!

Available from Harlequin Presents
February 2011

www.eHarlequin.com

HPI2972